Anonymous

Red Nosed Mike!

Confession of a terrible crime, assassination and robbery of Paymaster

McClure! and Hugh Flannaghan, on Wilkes-Barre Mountain

Anonymous

Red Nosed Mike!
Confession of a terrible crime, assassination and robbery of Paymaster McClure!
and Hugh Flannaghan, on Wilkes-Barre Mountain

ISBN/EAN: 9783337291297

Printed in Europe, USA, Canada, Australia, Japan

Cover: Foto ©Andreas Hilbeck / pixelio.de

More available books at **www.hansebooks.com**

RED NOSED MIKE!

Confession of a Terrible Crime,

ASSASSINATION AND ROBBERY OF

PAYMASTER McCLURE!

AND HUGH FLANNAGHAN, ON WILKES-
BARRE MOUNTAIN.

A History of the Crime!

As Exposed by

PINKERTON'S MEN.

Illustrations:

Red Nosed Mike in Jail--Scene Of the Murder.

The Escaped Murderers, Detectives, Etc.

WILKES-BARRE PA.
HART AND CO.. PUBS
1889.

AN ATROCIOUS CRIME.

Is It The Work Of The Italian Maifa?

TWELVE THOUSAND DOLLARS WAS THE PRIZE.

Cold Blooded and Deliberate Murder of Paymaster McClure and Hugh Flannaghan-- The Robbers Avoid Detection and two of them Flee to Italy--Michael Rezzelo, Alias Red-Nosed Mike, in Jail--Captain Linden, of Pinkerton's Men, Puts an Italian Detective on His Trail.

aring as the men of the Anthracite coal regions of Pennsylvania are, familiar with death in every form, including crushing, burning, explosions of fire damp, falling down deep shafts, and premature explosions of blasting powders in the mines, added to the ordinary accidents of railroading and chop employments, in cidental to the commercial and manufacturing interests of great and thriving business centres, so that death stalks abroad here red-handed in the open day, and his ghastly features are too familiar to excite more than passing notice as he makes his reckless demands upon human life; now in this hamlet, to-morrow in the town, and so, from day to day, he marches in an endless circuit striking down the young, the hopeful and the brave, as well as the old and decrepit; yet notwithstanding this easy and familiar acquaintanceship with death and all his subtle arts, the people of Wilkes-Barre and vicinity were horribly shocked on the morning of October 19, 1888, when the news spread abroad that two men had been foully murdered in the open day within a few miles of the city. Later on the fact became known that the object of the murder was the robbery of a paymaster who had drawn a large sum of money from one of the numerous banks in Wilkes-Barre that morning to pay the men who were engaged in constructing a new branch of the Lehigh Valley Railway, from Pleasant Valley to Fairview, on the eastern slope of Wilkes-Barre mountain. The boldness and swiftness of the murderers and robbers appalled the stoutest hearts; and strong men, familiar with the face of death as with their own, blanched as the particulars of the horrible crime were unfolded within an hour of its perpetration, and there was no longer room to doubt the awful certainty of the deed that robbed two light hearted, good natured men of their lives and the treasure entrusted to their care.

DISCOVERY OF THE VICTIMS.

Contractor James McFadden, of Philadelphia, who was engaged in constructing a section of the new Lehigh Valley branch, had established the rule to pay his men every cent due them on the 20th of every month and in pursuit of this rule, he despatched his book-keeper, J. Barney McClure and another trusty employe, Hugh Flannaghan to Wilkes-Barre on the morning of October 19th for the necessary funds to meet the demands of the following day. It was this never varying custom of the contractor to pay his men on the 20th of each and every month that made the planning of the robbery an easy matter, but as McClure had performed this same service regularly for many months without meeting with the slightest molestation or accident, there was no reason why the custom should be departed from on this occasion, it being the very last payment that the contractor would make, as the work was about completed and it only remained to pay the men the balance due them and break camp for a new job of railroad construction near Poughkeepsie, New York. Indeed, Mr. McFadden had completed his arrangements to leave on the morning of the 19th for Philadelphia, having given full instructions to his foreman and Paymaster McClure to pack and ship the tools to Poughkeepsie and go there themselves. As the hour approached at which Mr. McFadden should start for Wilkes-Barre in order to catch the train to Philadelphia he became uneasy. He knew that McClure should have arrived at the mountain office at half-past ten or thereabout at the farthest, but now 11 o'clock had struck and McClure was not yet in sight. Feeling that he could wait no longer and catch the train, Mr. McFadden stepped into his buggy at a few minutes after 11 o'clock and started down the only road leading from the wild and lonely mountain, knowing that McClure could not avoid meeting him on the way, unless delayed between the city and Miner's Mills, the first small village on the road to Wilkes-Barre. He had traversed about one mile of the loneliest road in Pennsylvania, when he discovered a horse standing in the road that he at once recognized as his paymaster's, apparently exhausted from recent exertion, and coupled with the fact that neither McClure or Flannaghan were in sight led him to conclude that the horse had ran away and thrown the two men from the buggy. Coming nearer, however, he

discovered the body of McClure lying under the wheels dead. He was horribly shocked at the awful sight. One foot had been caught in the side bar and the head and the upper portion of the body dragged on the ground. The young man was a great favorite of his and had left the camp that morning at 6 o'clock, full of life and spirit, in perfect health, and now he was still in death. It was some moments before McFadden, strong and powerful man as he was, could command his thoughts or actions and when he did finally recover a little, he turned his horse's head at once toward the construction camp in order to secure aid. Having arrived there, he

called his superintendent, Mr. McQuirn, and apprised him of the awful scene that he had witnessed down the road, but even then no suspicion of foul play had entered his mind, and he still believed that the horse had ran away. McQuirn did not accept this idea however, and at once inquired "if McFadden saw the money satchel in McClure's buggy?" "My gracious, when I come to think of it, no," answered the grief stricken contractor. "The satchel was not there!" "Then it is murder," said McQuirn. It required but a few minutes' time to return to the awful scene of the tragedy, and upon examination of McClure's body, Mr. McQuirn's suspicions were confirmed; as he tenderly removed the body from beneath the wheels, he pointed to two bullet holes in the back of the murdered man and thus all doubt as to the nature of the tragedy was at once removed. A closer examination of McClure's horse revealed the fact that the animal was also perforated with bullets and that his wounds must soon prove fatal. The two men sadly placed McClure's body in their own vehicle and at once started down the road in search of Flannaghan, whose body they found cold in death a quarter of a mile from where they took up the body of McClure. It was not mangled, but three bullet holes told the deadly work of the highwaymen. McQuirn then went on to Miner's Mills, where he told Postmaster Quigley of what had happened. The latter at once telephoned to County Detective Heffernan, Detective James O'Brien and the newspaper offices at Wilkes-Barre.

The detectives and a number of newspaper men at once started for Miner's Mills, where great excitement reigned. A number of the villagers, headed by Postmaster Quigley, went to the mountain as soon as McQuirn had told them the news. The bodies of the two dead men were placed in Quigley's grocery wagon and taken to Wisely's undertaking establish-

ment at Miner's Mills. Coroner Mahon had been telegraphed for and the bodies awaited his arrival. He did not arrive until 4 o'clock. McClure's body was horribly mangled from the dragging it received over the rough, rocky surface. Part of the skull was blown off and the supposition is that one of the murderers stood directly over him and fired, which lifted the roof of his head off. The brains oozed out and it was found necessary to gather them up and place them in a handkerchief. Flannaghan's death had been a clean and easy one. He was shot three times. One bullet struck him in the breast in the region of the heart which must have caused instant death itself. The other bullets lodged in the upper portion of the body also. Flannagan died where he fell. McClure was shot through the left eye and twice in the back.

CHAPTER II.

SEEKING CLUES.

Groups of men started out from a dozen different directions to the scene of the murder and within three hours hundreds of people had visited the scene and had formed as many different theories as to how and by whom the murders were committed. The detectives were followed closely by newspaper men and stood for hours viewing the scene of the first attack upon the paymaster and his assistant. The first object that attracted attention at the scene of the crime was a

LARGE POOL OF BLOOD

in the roadway. This was Flannaghan's life blood. Following the foot tracks visible in the road, the searchers came to the foot of a stately pine tree, the lower portion of which was hidden from view by thick underbrush. It was evident from the trampled down condition of the grasses and leaves at the foot of this tree, that the assassins had there taken their stand and waited a long time for the coming of their victims. The location was an excellent one for viewing the road from both sides, and a better selection could not have been made. From behind the tree one can see the road leading from Miner's Mills for a distance of 150 feet. This view gave the murderers a good chance to level their firearms and take accurate aim at their victims. The view up the road is not so good and can be seen only for a distance of about 75 feet. On the opposite side of the roadway from where the brigands lay in wait is another

large tree which was pierced by three heavy slugs. The bullets still remained in the tree but were cut out by the detectives.

The following diagram illustrates the scene of the attack:

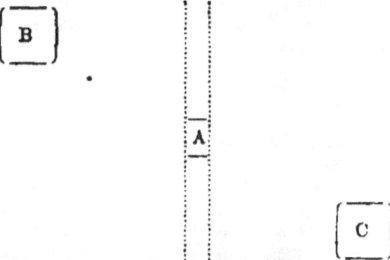

A—The spot in roadway where Flannagan's body was found. B—Tree on opposite side of road pierced with bullets. C—The tree behind which the murderers were concealed.

After gathering every possible clue at the scene of the murder, the detectives turned their attention to tracing the course of McClure and Flannaghan from the time they arrived in Wilkes-Barre until they left Miner's Mills on their journey to untimely graves. They found that Paymaster J. B. McClure and Hugh Flannaghan had left their mountain railroad camp at 6 o'clock in the morning as stated above and arrived in Wilkes-Barre at about 8 o'clock. It was before banking hours, and the two men put up their horse at McDonald's livery stable on Butler Alley, in Wilkes-Barre, and started out to call upon a few acquaintances during the hour's time that must elapse before they could secure the funds they were to draw from the bank. The pay-master had made no less than 12 similar trips before, and had never met with a mishap. On each of these trips McClure was accom-panied by Alexander McQuirn, who works under McFadden, who acted as a sort of body guard. But on Thursday Contractor Mc-Fadden issued an order that the superintend-ent and paymaster should not be absent from the work at the same time; that while one was away the other should remain. This order saved McQuirn's life. When McClure found he could not take the superintendent along he made arrangements with Hugh Flannaghan, the stable boss, to accompany him. A little after nine o'clock the paymaster called at the Wyoming National Bank and got his money—$12,000 in all, which he placed in a hand satchel. He then started for McDonald's liv-ery to get his rig. On his way he stepped into McLaughlin's cafe where he chatted very pleasantly for about ten minutes with the proprietor, Mr. McLaughlin. McClure com-plained of feeling cold and Mr. McLaughlin suggested that he get him a cup of hot coffee. The paymaster thought that would be just the thing and the coffee was forthcoming. While drinking the same McClure had the satchel in front of him on the table. Mr. McLaughlin picked it up and said, "My gracious, you must have quite a load in there; it is heavy."

McClure replied: "Oh, no, that isn't heavy. I have carried heavier loads than that; we have got only a small pay to-morrow and be-sides I told the cashier not to load me down with silver, but to give me all the notes he could. And he did. I have only got $345 in silver." The contents of the satchel were made up as follows: $2,000 in $50 bills, $3,500 in $20 bills, $3,000 in $10 bills, $2,000 in $5 bills, $1,155 in $1 and $2 bills, $300 in 25 and 50 cent pieces, $25 in 10 cent pieces, $10 in 5 cent pieces and $10 in pennies. Continuing the conversation, Mr. McLaughlin said:

"Well, who is going with you?"

"My friend, Hughy Flannaghan," was the reply.

Mr. McLaughlin.—"What, only two of you, that ain't enough, you ought to have a half dozen men. I have been up through that country hunting and don't think I would like to go through it with $12,000 in my posses-sion unless I had a large body guard."

McClure.—"Oh I don't mind it, Billy; you see I have a big shooter here with me and if I am attacked I can defend myself and besides Hughey is a fighter from away back." After chatting a few moments longer with

Mr. McLaughlin in pleasant social way, Mc-Clure started for McDonald's livery stables, where Flannaghan had already gone to get the horse and conveyance ready for their return trip. As the two men were about to drive away, McDonald looked at his watch and noted the time at 15 minutes to 10 o'clock. Mr. McDonald shook hands with McClure and laughingly said, "take care of the boodle, Mack." McClure said he would look after that. At 20 minutes after 10 the two men arrived at Quigley's store, Miner's Mills. McClure got out and went into Quigley's to inquire if there was any mail matter there for Mr. McFadden. Postmaster Quigley waited on the young paymaster and after he got his mail asked him to take a cigar. McClure de-clined with thanks, saying he was in a hurry to get back to the works. When McClure came out of the store he told Flannaghan to drive up quick as the "old man" (McFadden) might want to see him (McClure) before he left the works. The paymaster jumped into the buggy and away the two men sped up the mountain road. This was the last time friendly eyes looked upon the two men alive. An hour later as before stated, Contractor McFadden found them dead in the road.

NO SUBSTANTIAL CLUE.

The detectives were thoroughly thwarted in securing a clue from anything they might have been able to find on the ground as the anxious crowd that assembled at the scene were unmindful of the fact that every foot print they made in the road was but covering the tracks of the assassins. They had many different theories as to who committed the crime. No arrests were made, however, and the public and Contractor McFadden, especially, were sorely disappointed that some clue was not discovered whereby the detectives could place their hands upon the perpetrators of the foul deed at once and while their hands were yet covered with the uncongealed blood of their victims. Detective James O'Brien, special officer of the Lehigh Valley Railroad, advanced the most rational explanation of the crime, and all subsequent developments have borne out his views of the killing and the surround-ing circumstances. He expressed the opinion that no train robber from the west or thief from the large cities had a hand in the killing for the reason that the American robber never sheds human blood or takes human life until his own life is absolutely in danger, and even then he prefers to wound and disable to out-right killing. American highwaymen would have thrown a log or old tree across the road and while the wagon was halted to remove the obstruction the order to "hold up their

MICHAEL REZZELO.

MICHAEL REZZELO, *alias* Red Nosed Mike, the first of the murderous gang of
Italians placed on trial for the slaughtering of Paymaster J. B. McClure
and his assistant, Hugh Flannaghan, on Wilkes-Barre Mountain, October 19, 1888. Mike's trial began at Wilkes-
Barre Thursday, Feb. 7, 1889, and lasted until
the following Monday; the jury finding him guilty of murder in the
first degree, after a brief
consultation.

hands" would have been given, but until these means failed to bring the victims to terms, extreme measures would not be resorted to. No such merciful course was pursued in the murder of McClure and Flannaghan. The murderers shot down their victims without a word of warning. Another point worthy of notice was the fact that Flannaghan was pierced by three bullets, each and either of which would have been fatal. The distance at which these shots must have been fired, showed skill in marksmanship but when the body of McClure was examined by Coroner Mahon he found that two bullets had been fired into his back within an inch of each other. If conclusive evidence were needed that skillful hands did the shooting this fact settled it beyond all doubt. This evidence was the only clue so far obtained by the detectives. There is probably not a wilder or more desolate spot in the state than where the terrible tragedy was committed. There is not a house or any kind of habitation within a mile, and a whole regiment of men might be shot down and the outside world would not know of it for the time being. The woodland is covered with heavy underbrush, which made the work of the searchers difficult in the extreme. It was almost impossible to make any headway after one got in the woods. This aided the murderers materially to escape. The murderers were shrewd enough not to take any of the belongings of their victims which might lead to their detection. McClure's gold watch was found in the roadway and also all his private papers. To show how deliberate the murderers were and what excellent judgment they used, it is only necessary to state that they selected a point in the lonely road which would bring the horse up to where they were on a walk. In other words, the horse had to climb a steep incline, and it was natural to suppose that he would walk it rather than trot. This gave the marksmen an ambush an excellent opportunity to take steady aim and fire. There were other places in the nook which were more isolated than the spot selected, but they were on a dead level which would give the horse a chance to let himself out, and he was just that kind of a horse that would do it. It was no trouble for him at all to trot a mile in 3 minutes.

THE CORONER ARRIVES.

Coroner Dr. Mahon of Pittston arrived upon the scene in the evening and empaneled the following jury: P. T. Norton, John T. Moore, Esq., Michael Athey, Michael Mayock T. F. Quigley and Thomas Ryan. The jury viewed the remains and Coroner Mahon requested Dr. Matlack, of Miner's Mills, to perform the autopsy and adjourned the hearing.

SUSPICION FALLS UPON HUNTERS.

The fact that the shooting of McClure and Flannaghan was performed by good marksmen led the residents of Miner's Mills to look around upon the residents of that vicinity with careful scrutiny. Two brothers named Mock were known to be capital shots and the eye of suspicion was turned upon them by their neighbors. They were placed under

surveillance by the officers of the law, but as they were able to prove their presence elsewhere, during the morning of October 19th, they were finally discharged. Several other arrests were made but none of them were grounded upon well founded suspicion until Michael Rezello, alias "Red Nosed Mike" was placed under arrest by officer Roberts, on Nov. 3d. The arrest was rather premature, however, as the Pinkerton men had a theory as to who committed the crime but had determined to avoid making arrests until they had good substantial proofs of the guilt of the accused. The Pinkerton men and other officers of the law held a conference after Mike's arrest and determined upon a course of procedure that in the end brought out just what they were in search of. The newspapers of Wilkes-Barre only expressed the suspicions of every thinking citizen when they stated that the murder and robbery was the work of Italian brigands who had secured employment under contractor McFadden, along with hundreds of others of their countrymen in the construction of the new Lehigh Valley branch. It was argued by the papers that the habit of first

KILLING THEIR VICTIMS

was a characteristic of the bandits of Italy and especially of the bandits known as the Mafia, an

CAPT. ROBERT T. LINDEN.

CAPTAIN ROBERT T. LINDEN, of Pinkerton's men. To Captain Linden's skill and energy is chiefly due the credit of planning the trapping of Rezzelo. He was the prosecutor in the case against Mike, and showed great ability in preparing the testimony of himself and Pinkerton's men.

old Sicilian band of cutthroats that had distributed itself all over that country about the 12th century and that still exists and terrorizes the peasantry and poorer classes of Italy. It is known to also exist in this country and is a powerful aid to the Italian coiners and counterfeiters that;to–day infests every state and city in the United States.

MIKE DISCHARGED.

That the officers had a perfect understanding in reference to the whole matter was made evident as soon as he was brought before Squire Moore for a hearing. The officers themselves became Mike's warmest defenders against the awful charge and fairly wept in sympathy with him while he was held under suspicion. Postmaster Quigley, of Miner's Mills, acted as Mike's counsel at the hearing and examined the witnesses appearing for the people with such gusto as to convince Mike that there was not a shadow of suspicion against him. Mr. Roberts, who caused Mike's arrest, had his case well prepared and, although it was weak, he made the best of it.

Stephen Zink, clerk at Quigley's store, was the first witness; noticed nothing unusual about Mike's movements on the morning of the murder. In reply to cross question said Mike was not uneasy.

Henry F. Wilson, teamster, was on road that morning; met Mike and three other Italians; Mike was alone and when witness saw

him 500 yards from scene of murder; 175 yards further on met McClure. Witness said the first two Italians acted suspicious; they were in a hurry, walked fast; shouted to one; he hid his face, put his hand in hip pocket.

George Deeter, engineer at Oliver's Powder Mill, said the prisoner once asked him what they would do to a man in this country if he murdered another, and whether if he escaped to the old country they could bring them back Mike said he could kill a man and escape to a large city. Capt. Linden cornered the witness badly. Mr. Oplinger, of Miners' Mills; thought Mike resembled Italian who came to his house and asked about buying rifle. Next day two Italians showed witness new rifle, didn't think Mike was one of them.

J. S. Elston, Thomas Richardson and T. A. Kemball, of Plains, said they saw a man pass through Plains one August night with a rifle which he wanted to sell. Kimball swore positively that Mike was the man. Mr. Quigley said he could prove Mike was not in the county in August. No other arrests were made and so far as the public was concerned the matter was permitted to drop. Nothing more was heard of the case until the morning of January 2d, when the electric wires flashed the news all over the world that Pinkerton's men had arrested Mike and that they had secured a confession from him showing how and by whom the crime had been committed.

CHAPTER III.

HOW THE CRIME WAS COMMITTED.

The morning of October 19th, 1888, was wet and drizzly. This kind of weather favored the plans of the robbers who know that several wood choppers would be engaged at their employment of clearing the land about half a mile from the scene of their contemplated crime. Following the course pursued by Mike on the morning of the murder as developed at his first hearing before Squire Moore, and also as shown by his confession a reference to the following map of the roads leading to the spot where the crime was committed will convey a good idea of Mike's course on the morning of the murder.

MICHAEL REZELLO.

made his appearance at Quigley's store and post office at Miner's Mills at about 9:30 o'clock and talked freely with the clerk shewing no trepidation or excitement. He left the store at about 10 o'clock and proceeded up the road over which the intended victims would soon follow. On the way up Mike passed a farmer named Wilson who was

driving towards Miner's Mills. Had Mike been a sharp fellow capable of weighing his surroundings or seeing in this meeting with farmer Wilson a powerful link in the chain of circumstantial evidence that he began to link around himself the moment he appeared at Quigley's store that morning and knowing what his own intentions and those of his pals where he would have turned back and warned the paymaster of his danger. Mike, it appears, had formed an idea of the law requirements of evidence necessary to convict for murder in his own mind, and his wily companions led him on to the fatal trip. Mike believed when he confessed the part he took in the crime, that the major part of the deed having been performed by his companions, he would escape with light punishment. On no other ground can his want of ordinary cunning be accounted for. Mike may have also been led to believe by his companions that when they fled the country and escaped with the money that he would be safe in confessing the small part he took in the crime.

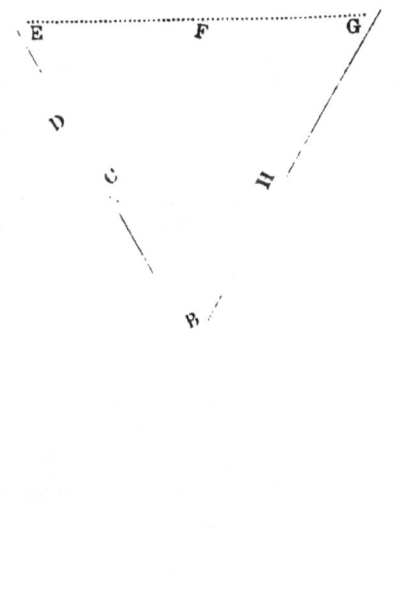

A—Miner's Mills. B—Place where Mike was overtaken by his victims on morning of murder. C—Stump of tree where Bevevino stood and fired first shot at McClure. D—Villella's position when he shot Flannaghan. E.—Where Contractor McFadden found horse. F—Course pursued by robbers after murder to reach Mike's shanty at G. H.—White House road.

But this idea could only be imposed upon a very weak minded man, and such a man Mike Rezello has proven himself to be. Else, as stated above his head would have warned him to desist, even though his heart felt no pulse of mercy to a man who had befriended him. But Mike was not capable of realizing anything but the fact that a great pile of treasure would soon be within his grasp.

When Mike reached the fork of the White House road and turned his head back he could see down the road 500 feet. The presumption is that he walked very fast from the point where Farmer Wilson met him to the White House road and it is also the belief that Mike had entered upon the straight stretch of road where McClure's horse turned the bend and entered the same stretch. Mike, walking, could easily have heard the horse's footstep and the noise of the carriage behind. It was his intention to reach a bend in the White House road before McClure came upon the home stretch. Had he reached this bend he could have easily made his way through the skirting of woods where his pals lay in wait without attracting attention. It is known that this was his intention because he did not want McClure to see him, fearing lest the shooting was not successful that he might be detected. But when he saw McClure's horse had already turned the bend in the lower part of the road he made no effort to reach the White House road. He could have done it had he ran, but he did not dare to do this lest it arouse McClure's suspicion. The Italian then walked along leisurely until McClure's team came up to him. Mike did not have the presumption to hang his head down when McClure passed, because that would have caused the good and open hearted Barney to ask "what was the matter with Michael this morning?" A little delay and a few words of conversation just then might have turned the whole aspect of affairs. The murderous heart within Mike's breast might have wilted, and the lives of the two men saved. But such was not to be the case. Mike did look up and give a grunt in answer to McClure's salutation, "hello, Mike."

Eight hundred yards further up the road is the famous black tree stump behind which Bevevino stood when he fired his fatal shot at McClure. The stump is nearly all cut away now by relic hunters. The party then took a see-saw cut through the forest for two miles, coming out at the new railroad. There is no question but that had the highwaymen met anybody in the woods that morning they would have shot them dead, as identification was equal to death for the murderers. The road through the woods is stubby and rocky, and an ordinary pedestrian could not make very good time in his travels. After the murderers reached the railroad they were safe, as trains were not running yet, and there were no strangers to question their movements. Passing down the railroad 200 feet the murderers made their way down the steep embankment which leads to the old Kelly creek road overlooking the deep ravine on the left. In the distance, towards Parsons, can be plainly seen the first dam of the Wilkes-Barre Water Company. Beyond the ravine is Mountain Park about half a mile straight across. To the right of the road is a high cliff of rocks covering an area of three fourths of an acre. Some of these overhanging rocks would weigh 40 tons. In order to reach the pinnacle of top rock you must climb over a number of smaller ones. It is a tedious job and unless you were a regular Alp climber you would have no desire to run the risk of

have caused them to look around in fear.

The rock under which the money was secreted is 800 feet distant from the first cut off, north of Kelly's Creek. This cut was driven through by Robert Petrello (Mike's brother-in-law) who had one section and William Deverex. Petrello employed all Italians and they were familiar with every foot of ground for miles around. Nearly all of them had revolvers and on Sundays and wet days they would practice target-shooting. Near Mike's shanty, now demolished, was

[Mike's Shanty.]

breaking your bones in order to gratify your legs. On one of the mammoth rocks is a large tree which seems to grow out of the rock itself, so thoroughly imbued is it in the hardened surface. Abutting this rock is just as large a companion and noble, and at the bottom where nature has failed to bring them in contact is a large crevice. A man could crawl into this opening. No better spot could be selected for hiding the stolen bag and the shrewdness and cunning of the murderers is amply testified to by the fact that that they went out of their way such a long way to store the money. There is not one man in a thousand who would have imagined for a moment that the bandits carried their booty so far. The supposition would be, and was, that the treasure was buried somewhere in the woods near the scene of the tragedy. But here again is where the cunning of the murderers came in. They knew if they buried the money near the scene of the shooting a search would be made; and also that when the thieves returned to claim their stolen property they would run the risk of being detected. Hence to avoid all obstacles they carried the satchel two miles over the mountains where it would be near at hand when wanted. The distance from Red Nose Mike's shanty to the hiding place in the rocks is about 400 yards. One night when it rained in torrents the murderers visited the cave in the rock, where, with the aid of a bulls-eye lantern, they divided their blood-stained greenbacks. Even though the hearts of the villains were as hard as iron and their conscience as thick as a stone wall, a terrible feeling must have come over the cowards that night as they sat in silence and apportioned the money. Every sound of the wind must

found cans of every description. Every one of them were riddled with bullets. This is the way the Italian and Hungarian railroaders amuse themselves on Sundays and holidays. It is a fact well known to all business men in the vicinity where such laborers are employed that the first thing they buy is a revolver and next a trunk to keep it in. That's all the use they ever have for the trunk.

HOW MIKE WAS CAUGHT.

A countryman of Mike's, Francisco De Luska, who has been known in connection with the case as the "Italian Detective," is in the employ of the Pinkerton agency. His father is an Italian and his mother is believed to be of Irish descent. Francisco spent seven years in Europe and speaks the Italian language fluently. After Mike went to Poughkeepsie from this city, DeLuska was sent there at McFadden's suggestion, and put to work. He was instructed to make Mike's acquaintance, gain his confidence and become as intimate with him as possible. In this he experienced no difficulty. Mike took to him from the first and they were soon on the most intimate terms of friendship. DeLuska told him that he had been interpreter for an Italian on trial for a great crime. He had cleared the prisoner by false interpretation. This had been discovered and he was forced

THOS. FRANCIS QUIGLEY.

THOMAS FRANCIS QUIGLEY, Postmaster and business man of Miner's Mills,
who "had a theory of the crime," and who played his part
so well as to disarm Red Nose Mike's
suspicions.

to flee to escape the penalty of his offence. He sought Mike's assistance and protection. The story had its effect. Mike took kindly to the stranger.—companion as he seemed in evading the clutches of the law. They traveled together. Wherever Mike was, there was DeLuska almost certain also to be. After a few days, McFadden went over, and to carry out the plan previously arranged, took steps, through Mike, to secure a position for the stranger, in which the two should be even more closely associated than they had hitherto been. DeLuska had also asked Mike to intercede for him in the securement of a lucrative position, so that when McFadden declared himself to be dissatisfied with his present time-keeper and proposed to Mike that he take the position, the latter promptly responded that he could not fill the bill, but he would get some one who would. Mr. McFadden knew well that he could not do the work as he was unable to read or write English, and also that the "some one" to whom Mike referred was the "Italian detective." McFadden told him to go ahead. At Mike's request DeLuska was soon in his new position, he and Mike entering into an arrangement that he (Mike) and some of his friends should be given extra time occasionally, and if they lost any time they were not to be docked for it, the proceeds of this scheme to be divided between them. It was with this understanding that DeLuska assumed the duties of time-keeper. He had no money and wherever they went together—and they were together all the time—Mike footed all the bills, De Luska to pay him back at the end of the month. They went to Poughkeepsie a number of times. On two of these occasions Mike had a $50 bill changed at the bank and at another time they had one changed at a saloon of which a lady was the keeper. All this time the detective was keeping a close eye on Mike and the latter was boasting of the good time he was having with the new time keeper—increasing his wages through the little system of time-stealing that they had inaugurated and enjoying other privileges which a less considerate "boss" would not have allowed.

Finally DeLuska got an inkling that Mike contemplated leaving the country and going to Italy. Fearing that he might get away from him he persuaded him to accompany him to Philadelphia for a little trip, as he said, and to see some friends there. They went on Wednesday, the 2nd inst. They were met at the station in Philadelphia by Detective Dougherty, of the Pinkerton Agency, by whom DeLuska was at once arrested. Mike was loud in his protestations against the out-

rage, as he regarded the arrest, and demanded to know what it was for. He was informed that it was for the commission of a crime, whereupon Mike protested the Italian's innocence and declared that he was clear of all trouble. Detective Dougherty, however, was not satisfied, and took DeLuska back to Poughkeepsie. leaving Mike in charge of Captain Linden.

Mike was taken to the Captain's office, where, after the warrant for his arrest was read, Captain Linden addressed him as follows:

"Mike, the cashier of the Wilkes-Barre Bank, where Paymaster McClure got his money, says he had a mark on all of his bills, by which he could tell them. He says that the bill you had changed in the bank at Poughkeepsie has a mark on it and is one that the paymaster had in his satchel." The Captain then showed Mike a bill which he gave him to understand was the one referred to. The same process was gone through in regard to the other two bills changed at Poughkeepsie, the Captain producing each one and showing Mike the cashier's mark upon it.

At this the culprit weakened and made a complete confession, telling of his part in the crime, naming Guesseppa Bevivino and Vincenzo Vabala as his accomplices and telling where the gun, satchel and silver money were hidden, how the shooting was done, etc.

Captain Linden then produced what purported to be Mike's confession and he and the alderman held a private consultation, after which Captain Linden stated that the substance of the confession left no manner of doubt as to Mike's guilt but in order that the ends of justice be served he at this time would simply ask that Mike be committed until his officers could arrest the other parties to the crime. The committment was then made out and Mike was taken to Luzerne county prison in north Wilkes-Barre, where he will remain until he is tried and hanged for his awful crime.

This confession was taken down in writing and on Friday afternoon, January 4, Captain Linden and his assistant, Detective Frank C. Thayer, brought Mike to Wilkes-Barre. Under the cover of darkness—fearing that if they went in the daytime Mike would be lynched—they made the trip to the lonely spot on the mountain side, walking from Miner's Mills, and there, at the solemn hour of midnight, by the dim, flickering light of a miner's lamp. the arch villain pulled the things from their place of concealment and

J. B. McCLURE.

McClure, the paymaster and book-keeper for Contractor McFadden.
He was the only son of the late Major McClure,
of Philadelphia.

thus convinced the officers of the truth of his confessed connection with the horrible crime.

The following day Mike was brought before Squire Rooney and after a formal charge of murder had been entered by Captain Linden, Mike was asked what he had to say?

He answered, "I have nothing to say now. I will not talk until my friends come."

CHAPTER IV.

MIKE'S CONFESSION.

FTER Captain Linden had refused all requests of newspapermen to see Rezzelo's confession, Post-master Quigley, of Plains, called at the prison and as soon as Mike heard who it was that desired to see him seemed very glad of the opportunity to talk to Quigley whom he had come to look upon as a very dear friend. He showed no hesitancy whatever in answering the questions put by Mr. Quigley, as follows:

"The scheme to waylay and murder Paymaster McClure was first concocted on Sunday, Sept. 2. Greed for money was at the bottom of it all. We thought what a good time we would have in Italy if we could get the money. We talked over it for a long time and finally concluded to carry out the scheme. We looked over the woods thoroughly until we found a good place to hide our firearms and the money. After looking about for two months we finally found the place we were looking for. Then I bought a rifle at a store in Wilkes-Barre and we were ready. There were three of us. On the morning of Friday, October 19, I saw McClure away from the works. I then followed to Miner's Mills and stopped at Quigley's. Villella, alias Jim, and Bevivino did not come to Miner's Mills that morning; they remained in the woods.

Question by Quigley—Did McClure pass you between my place (Quigley's store) and the scene of the murder.

Answer—He did; just at the White House road, where I was supposed to have turned off to go to my shanty.

Quigley—"What did McClure say to you, if anything?"

Answer—He said: "Hello, Mike!"

Quigley—"What did you say?"

Answer—"I said hello, and nodded my head."

Quigley—"Then what followed?"

Answer—"As soon as McClure and Flannaghan passed me in the carriage I quickened my pace, but McClure and Flannaghan paid no attention to me; we were now close onto where the other two men lay in ambush and I began to get a little nervous."

Quigley—"Who fired the first shot?"

Answer—"The blacksmith Bevivino. He did the principal shooting. He was an expert shot. Bevivino was behind the stump of a tree on the right hand side of the road going up. You know the place very well Mr. Quigley; we went to see it right after the shooting. Villella stood upon the opposite side of the road. He shot Flannaghan. Quigley—Then I understood you to say that McClure was shot first and not Flannaghan.

Answer—"Yes, that's how it was, you thought however, that it was Flannaghan who was shot first.

Quigley—"Yes, that's what everybody thought."

Quigley—"Do I know your accomplices in the crime?"

Answer—"Yes, you know them well. Don't you know Villella? He's the fellow that quarrelled with you in front of your store when he was buying cabbage of a huckster. And the other fellow was with him, and don't you mind the day Bevivino bought the shoes off you?"

Mr. Quigley brought the two men to mind at once and he would know them in a crowd of a million people.

Quigley—"Where are these men now?"

Answer—"They are both in Italy; they left three weeks after the murder."

Quigley—"How far up the road was Villella from Bevivino?"

Answer—"About 50 yards."

Quigley—"When did you shoot?"

Answer—"I shot from the rear. I fired four shots altogether at the occupants of the carriage. After McClure and Flannaghan had been shot the horse started on a dead run. Villella got frightened and ran through the woods to his shanty. He deserted us without warning. At one time it looked as though the horse was going to get away and I thought we had killed the men for nothing. The blacksmith (Bevivino) was fleetfooted, however, and he ran after the horse at breakneck speed. He finally caught up to him and grabbed him by the reins. He then shot him in the head. Then he cut the strap that held

HUGH FLANNAGHAN.

HUGH FLANNAGHAN, the murdered stable boss, who accompanied Paymaster
McClure to Wilkes-Barre on the fatal day. No bullets were found
in his body, showing that he was shot by the Winchester Rifle
Seven thousand dollars in Pennsylvania State Government Bonds were found sewed in his clothing,
after the same was removed on the day
of his death. He was about 50
years old and of sandy
complexion.

the satchel fast to the carriage and hurried through the woods to the hiding place. I arrived at my shanty a little before 12 o'clock."

Quigley—"Then it is true what Farmer Lawler testified at the hearing before Squire Moore that when you came there your clothes were wet and you were excited?"

Answer—"Yes, my clothes were wet, but I was not excited; no more than I am now. I changed my clothes."

Quigley—"Did you see anything of Mr. McFadden on the road that morning?"

Answer—"No, but the probabilities are that had he appeared he would have been killed, too. We wouldn't have stopped in our work for one man."

Quigley—"I used to often hear at my store that Bevivino was such a good shot. Was he?

Answer—"Oh, yes, he was a splendid marksman; he was a gunsmith in Italy and knew everything about the different makes of firearms. I used to see him practicing shooting on the railroad."

Quigley—"After you got the satchel out of the carriage you left the team standing in the road, didn't you?"

Answer—"Yes."

Quigley—"When you went through the woods what road did you come out on to get to the shanty?"

Answer—"We took the White House road."

Quigley—"Then Mike, as I understand you you delayed at my place in the morning of the 19th for the purpose of watching McClure?"

Answer—"Yes, I waited until I thought it was about time for him to come."

Quigley—"When did the other Italians sail for the old country?"

Answer—"On the 24 of November."

Quigley—"What do you think your prospects are of getting clear of this scrape?"

Answer—"I think I'll get out all right,"

The prisoner asked Mr. Quigley to take a dispatch to the telegraph office. The telegram was addressed to his father at Stanfordsville.

CHAPTER V.

GATHERING IN MIKE'S PALS.

THE Pinkerton men knew that the murderers of McClure and Flannaghan had accomplices in Philadelphia who aided in the escape of Bevivino and Villalla to Italy. One week after Mike had confessed to Captain Linden in Philadelphia, the latter arrested Francisco Cheriosko as an accessory after the fact, having aided the fugitives from justice, to escape from the country. Cheriosko was at once brought to Wilkes-Barre and brought before Squire Rooney for a hearing. The Alderman's office was crowded. The prisoner occupied a seat between the two Pinkerton men and facing the justice. Ex-District Attorney Lenahan conducted the case for the Commonwealth. The prisoner stated that he was a dressmaker by occupation, and lived at 822 Washington avenue, Philadelphia. He knew Michael Rezzelo, alias Red Nose Mike, since the latter was a child. Witness also knew Villilla; first heard of the murder on the 24 of last November. This is the date, according to Mike's confession, that his co-partners in crime sailed for Italy. Mike

was the man who told witness about the murder; witness admitted that he had aided the murderers to escape the detectives and get out of the country; he aided them by correspondence and did this because he was afraid of the Italians lest they murder him. Witness did not receive any money directly from the murderers to aid their escape, but admitted that he had in his possession some money given him by Bevivino. Red Nose Mike afterwards asked for the money saying it was his; witness saw the letter from Mike asking for the money. Mike asked witness for Bevevino's address and he gave it to him; witness knew at time he received the money that the men who gave it to him were implicated in a murder.

Alderman Rooney considered this sufficient evidence to hold the man and he committed him. Captain Linden and Detective Thayer took him to jail.

On January 22d last, word was received by Pinkerton's men that the papers for the extradition of the two accomplices of Red Nose Mike, who took part in the cold blooded murder of Paymaster McClure and his assistant had been prepared and forwarded to the Italian Government. To avoid any danger of their making their escape before the arrival of the papers the authorities here cabled that government to hold them until such time as the papers might arrive. A reply to this was received later, also by cable, stating that

DE LUSKA SPOTTING THE ITALIANS.

FLEEING TO ITALY.

[REPORTERS IMPORTUNING DETECTIVES FOR NEWS.]

as soon as they entered and denied all comers an opportunity to hear what transpired. In a few moments the party again appeared and left for the county prison. The newspapers of the following day announced that Antonio Pretrello, Red-Nosed Mike's brother-in-law, had been arrested. But Captain Linden denied the truth of this statement and refused to make public the name of the unknown until the time of Mike's trial arrived. Then, said he, I will go upon the stand and tell who the prisoner is. Until that time on one can know, as such information at this time would defeat the ends of justice. Failing here, the reporters visited the jail and demanded to see the prison docket, but Warden Brockway would neither permit them to see the docket or the prisoner and the last arrest is now known as t e Unknown. He is a young man of 23 years.

the request could not be complied with, the Italian government not deeming a charge made by telegraph sufficient ground upon which the accused could be held. This fact was discounted by the American Consul who will see that the men are identified and held until Pinkerton's men arrive in Italy and produce documentary evidence of their guilt.

THE "UNKNOWN" IN JAIL.

On January 24, in the early morning Francesco De Luska was observed entering the Exchange Hotel, Public Square, Wilkes-Barre, with a strange Italian. Word went out at once that another of the McClure and Flannaghan murders was in custody. Reporters were soon as thick as bees at the hotel office in less than an hour and were straining every nerve to get a glimpse of the new arrest, but Captain Linden, who had arrived about this time would give no information as to who his prisoner was. He at once proceeded to the private room where De Luska and his companion were in seclusion waiting for the Captain to appear. What transpired within the room no one was able to learn, but the supposition was that the "unknown" had been making a statement and that De Luska interpreted the sam_ "bile Captain Linden formulated the same in r.n 'sh. After remaining in the room for the space . i an hour the party left the hotel and started for the office of Squire Rooney, who locked his court

WHO THE VICTIMS WERE.

The young paymaster, J. Barney McClure, was a round-featured, smooth-faced man, 23 years old. He had been in the employ of Contractor McFadden since he left school and was the only son of his widowed mother. His father, the late well-known soldier, Major McClure, won his epaulets in the civil war for distinguished service on the side of the Union. There are two sisters of the deceased, however, who are abundantly able to care for their aged and invalid mother, who resides at Downingtown, Chester County, Pa. They are both married to prosperous business men. Young McClure was to have been married in

MC CLURE'S HOME AT DOWINGTOWN.

j ust two weeks from the day he was murdered to a most estimable young lady in Philadelphia. In preparation for the happy event the young man had ordered a suit of clothes from one of Wilkes-Barre's leading tailors. Alas, for the sad ending of all his hopeful, joyous plans. The suit he was to have been wed in proved to be his shroud. His genial, pleasant manners, free from guile or deceit made him a desirable companion for either man or woman, and a large circle of acquaintences throughout Wilkes-Barre and his native town mourned his loss as though he had been their own kindred. His remains was removed to his late home and was buried beside his father in the family plot near Downingtown.

Hugh Flannaghan was one of those droll clear-headed Irishmen that inspire confidence and security by their presence. He was a bachelor and a standing joke among his familiars was that he was laying away a long stocking full of golden sovereigns that he would some day take back to Ireland with him to his native hills in Donegal and lay at the feet of the darling colleen he left behind while he sought wealth on America's friendly shores. Hugh was a sober, quiet man, free from bad habits and stood high in the esteem of all who knew him. When his clothing was searched $7,000 in U. S. Government bonds were found upon his person. He had no known relatives in this country and was about 45 years old at the time of his death. His remains were interred in St. Mary's cemetery, Hanover, near Wilkes-Barre.

BASE INGRATITUDE.

When Contractor McFadden commenced work on the new Lehigh Valley Railroad here, Joe Perrio was the Italian leader who furnished the Italian laborers for the work. He was an intelligent man, shrewd and possessed of good business tact. He held aloof from the common tribe of his countrymen so to speak, and while not superintending his business affairs in this section, was in New York and Philadelphia, looking after other interests. The day after the crime he was at the Lehigh Valley depot and his handsome appearance attracted considerable attention. Perrio's headquarters were at Yatesville and from there he sent out all supplies to the Italians working on the railroad. He purchased his goods at wholesale and charged the highest prices. He never lost a cent as all of his bills were turned into the paymaster's office monthly. It is estimated that Perrio made $600 clear every month. Red Nose Mike, who was only a clerk at Robert Petrello's boarding house, was jealous of Perrio's great success and frequently carried stories, detrimental to him, to Superintendent McQuirn and Paymaster McClure. In the course of time these stories had their effect and McClure and McQuirn soured on Perrio.

They used their influence with Contractor McFadden and succeeded in having Perrio displaced as general sutler for the Italian laborers. McClure then went to Rezzelo and told him that when the road at Poughkeepsie was begun, he (Mike) could have Perrio's place. Mike was elated over this and would have a chance to make lots of money. This was fully two months before the murder took place. The question now arises, "what prompted Mike to show such ingratitude to the men who had befriended him?" At the time McClure had offered Mike this lucrative place the latter had already entered into a conspiracy to kill him. Why he consented to carry out the conspiracy in face of the fact that his material prosperity in the future was guaranteed is a mystery that cannot be solved. The only explanation given is that the fiend now in the county jai is a brute in human form. Some may say, probably Mike's confederates in crime would have squealed had he failed to carry out the plot. But this is not likely, as Mike's companions in crime were his cousins and he could have greatly benefitted them when he secured Perrio's fortune.

THE GREAT TRIAL.

---o-o---

Red-Nosed Mike Guilty in the First Degree.

---o-o---

STARTLING INCIDENTS OF THE LONG MURDER TRIAL.

---o-o---

The Prisoner Breaks Down and Weeps--He Confirms His Former Confession to Quigley and Detective Linden--The Jury Find a Verdict of Murder in the First Degree After an Absence of 55 Minutes--Closing Scenes.

---o-o---

N THE history of Luzerne County criminal court no event has aroused as much public interest as did the case of Michael Rezzelo, and from the time the Court House at Wilkes-Barre was opened on Monday until his trial began on Thursday, standing room could not be had for either love or money. The corridors leading to the large court chamber were crowded long before the hour fixed for court to convene, and good-natured crowds jostled each other throughout the day, vainly endeavoring to come near enough to the doors to get a peep in at the court and the prisoner. Three cases of murder had been tried during the week and each trial had resulted in an acquittal. The public began to get uneasy as to the possible outcome in Mike's case and this impression was confirmed on Tuesday, when his counsel, Gen. W. H. McCartney, stood up in court and requested a further

postponement of his client's trial on the ground that he had not had time to look over the evidence and to summon witnesses from a distance. Judge Charles E. Rice was on the bench, and after hearing Gen. McCartney's plea for delay, denied the request, and stated that the trial must go on. Gen. McCartney then resigned as counsel for Rezzelo, after making the point that Captain Linden, the prosecutor in the case, had several times asked for a postponement and had his request granted. 'Now," he continued, "the accused gives good reasons why the delay asked for should be granted, but there is no postponement to be had." The Court thereupon appointed Attorneys E. A. Lynch and John Garman as counsel for the accused and informed them that the trial would follow on Thursday of the present week (Feb. 7.)

There was, therefore, a great crowd of anxious people at the Court House doors on Thursday morning and long before 9 o'clock, a. m., had struck, the corridors were literally packed with people bent on hearing Mike's trial. A sensational case of "finding a father for the child of a young woman from the country" took up the time of the court until

11:45 o'clock, at' which time the Judge charged the jury, and they had no sooner retired than Michael Rezzelo was called to answer to the charge of murder and Captain Linden, of Pinkerton's detectives, was called to the prosecutor's table. The interest of the audience became intense as the accused and his counsel took their places at the defendant's table. The interest was doubly increased a moment later, if that were possible, as the two lawyers, after a moment's consultation arose and approached the Judge's bar and moved for a continuance of the case, Mr. Lynch pleading want of time to properly pre pare the case, as none of the important witnesses for his client had been served with notice to attend. They lived many miles away; some at Philadelphia and others at Poughkeepsie, N. Y. He and Mr. Garman had come into the case but a day or two before and it was unreasonable to ask them to proceed with the defense while there was nothing done to bring that defense forward at this time. They had called upon Mike at the jail as soon as they were appointed as his counsel and learned for the first time time that Mike had a father at Poughkeepsie, to whom he had written on January 20th for the means to defray the expenses of his trial and his father had promised to send money as soon as he could sell a house that he owned. Mike had also informed Gen. McCartney of these facts and did not know that McCartney was not going to secure a postponement of the case until now. A dispatch was also read from Mike's father in reply to one sent by Mike yesterday, in which he stated he would be here to-day. Mr. Lynch also maintained that the alleged confession or statement which the detectives had received of Mike was of benefit to the Commonwealth, in that it led to the identity of the other parties to the crime and enabled the State to pursue them. For these reasons he was entitled to consideration and should be given ample opportunity to defend himself against the charge upon which he was arraigned.

District Attorney Dart, in opposing the motion, stated that there had been no neglect on the part of defendant's counsel, but there had been on the part of the defendant himself. There had been ample time for him to prepare for his defense. the case having been down for trial at different times and continued.

Mr. Garman claimed that the defendant had not been negligent. He had relied upon his counsel, General McCartney, and had not known until yesterday, that he had withdrawn from the case. Then, too, Mike is ignorant and was not really cognizant of his real situation and of the circumstances surrounding him.

The District Attorney here stated that he understood that General McCartney said the agreement between himself and Mike was not kept by the latter.

MIKE CALLED UP.

Mr. Lynch then called Mike before the bar and he testified to the truth of the statements of his counsel as above set forth, and also named Mrs. Kemmerer, Harry Stetzer, John Miles and other residents of Philadelphia as important witnesses, who have known him for a long time, and that he regarded their presence as essential to his interests in the case. He further said these people would come here if notified, and reitered the statement of counsel that he did not know General McCartney had withdrawn and supposed he was attending to his interests, and would secure a postponement. He also said that since his imprisonment he had no money, but about a dollar, and could not send for witnesses or pay for the serving of the processes.

JUDGE RICE DENIES MOTION.

Judge Rice listened patiently and with every degree of respect to the pleadings of Mike's counsel, but failed to see in their arguments any good legal ground for a further postponement of the case. He was certain that the interests of the defendant would be well taken care of by the able counsel which had been appointed to conduct his case, and that they would secure him a fair trial. This was all anyone could do. The motion for a postponement was then formerly denied.

Mr. Lynch immediately asked the privilege of filing a written motion before the jury was drawn, and this was granted. He immediately went to work preparing it.

The written motion above alluded to was filed just before the noon adjournment. It was as follows:

Commonwealth vs. Michael Rezzello.	In Oyer and Terminer, Luzerne County, Indictment murder and manslaughter.

Now, Feb. 7, 1889, comes the defendant in above cases by his attorneys, E. A. Lynch and J. M. Garman, and moves to quash the array of jurors in above case for that the order of the court direct that 1550 names shall be selected as jurors for the year 1889, whereas a careful count shows that there are 1554 names upon the roll for 1889 which is contrary to order of Court, and to the statute in such cases made and provided.

2. For that the oath of the Sheriff and Jury Commsssioners is required by law to be reduced to "writing and filed in the office of

CAPT. ALFRED C. DARTE.

DISTRICT ATTORNEY ALFRED C. DARTE, who conducted the trial of Michael Rezzelo.

the Prothonotary of Luzerne county," whereas said oath is a printed form and not in compliance with the Act of Assembly.

EDWARD A. LYNCH,
JOHN M. GARMAN,
Attorneys for Michael Rezzelo.

Court then adjourned until 2 o'clock p. m. for dinner.

At 2 o'clock when the afternoon session opened, everything was confusion while the crowd surged into the court room, battled with the tipstaves, and climbed on the window sills on the outside. When order was restored, Mr. Garman argued the motion previously made, to quash the array of jurors. The certificates from the Jury Commissioners were presented, as also the additional list. The District Attorney said that no harm would result to the defendant by their being more than the usual number of jurymen on the panel. Attorney Lenahan claimed that the discrepancy was not so great as to be material. Judge Rice finally overruled the motion.

Mr. Lynch then placed the following before the court:

Michael Rezzolo, the defendant in the above case, being duly sworn, says: That as he is informed and verily believes that he cannot obtain a fair trial at this time in this county, by reason of the fact that there is undue excitement among the people thereof against him; and he further states and believes that there exists in the county great prejudice against him so that he cannot obtain a fair trial. He therefore requests the court to grant him a rule to take the testimony of witnesses to prove the above state of facts before ordering him to trial in this county. All of which he verily believes he will be fully able to establish to the satisfaction of the court.

And he will ever pray, etc.

MICHAEL REZZOLO.

District Attorney Darte thought here, as well as in any other county, the accused could get a fair trial.

The court would not grant the rule to show cause why a change of venue should not be made.

Mr. Lynch asked time to prepare evidence in support of it, but it was not allowed him.

Mr. Garman moved again to quash the array of jurors on other grounds—on the fact that some of the jurymen were now non-residents of the county, and also that some are dead, thus reducing the number below 1550. This motion was also overruled. Availing themselves of every possible loophole by which they could gain their point, they asked that the array of grand jurymen be also quashed. This, too, was immediately denied them.

Everything was now in readiness for the trial. Mike was told to stand up. Capt. Darte read to him the indictment, charging him with murder in the first degree. When the words were addressed to him, "What do you say to the charge?" he shook his head and said "No." The call of jurors then, at 3:15, was commenced.

After calling 58 jurymen the necessary 12 were selected, as follows:

Joseph R. Hart, druggist, Wilkes-Barre.

C. H. Mahon, agent, Pittston.

G. W. Strong, merchant, Pittston.

Thomas B. Miller, book agent, Wilkes-Barre.

W. G. Jaquish, carpenter, Luzerne Borough.

Daniel Keiper, surveyor, Dennison township.

S. C. Manderville, farmer, Lehman.

Chas. Cox, miner, Lehman.

J. B. Caubagh, teacher, Freeland.

Wm. Clinger, carpenter, Butler.

James Schatzle, blacksmith, White-Haven.

The call then proceeded until the panel was exhausted and the calling of those previously stood aside was begun. The first man called was accepted and the jury was completed by the swearing in of

Thomas Silvers, slater, Nanticoke.

The usual hour for evening adjournment having arrived Judge Rice warned the jury to be extremely careful not to mention anything about the case; he then adjourned court until the following day, Friday Feb. 8th, at 9 o'clock a m.

CHAPTER VII.

SECOND DAY OF THE TRIAL.

Friday morning having dawned cold and clear the scenes around the Court House of previous days were surpassed by the frantic efforts of the public to secure seats at the great trial. Policemen and tipstaves loomed up into momentary importance that in the eyes of those bent upon securing good places placed them on a higher plane of authority than the Judge on the bench, for he might give comfort to the members of the Court, while the tipstaves could give comfort to those whose needs could only be met and served by the fellow who sat, club in hand, without the bar of justice, and who represented the very toes of the law, so to speak.

At 9 o'clock Deputy Sheriff P. M. Conniff brought in the prisoner, Michael Rezzolo, and

CHAS. McFADDEN, ESQ.

JAMES O'BRIEN.   T. J. HEFFERNAN.

CHARLES McFADDEN, ESQ., contractor and railroad builder, of Phiadelphia,
who employed young McClure and Flannaghan, the
victims of the Italian Murderers.

——o——

JAMES O'BRIEN, special detective of the Lehigh Valley Railway Company, at
Wilkes-Barre. Messrs. O'Brien and Heffernan worked together
in bringing many of the crimes committed in Luzerne
County of late years to light.

——o——

THOMAS J. HEFFERNAN, County Detective, of Luzerne County, under administration of District Attorney James L. Lennahan. Mr.
Heffernan rendered valuable aid in the
conviction of Rezzelo.

placed him at the defendant's table beside his counsel. Michael was accompanied by his father and sister, the latter a little girl of perhaps 11 summers while his father had the appearance of a man of 50 years old. Mike's little sister gazed about at the sea of faces and as she looked into the eyes bent upon her, and hers, her young soul seemed to melt under the magnetic blaze of the hundreds of eyes that revealed to her innocent heart that her brother was already within the grasp of death and within sight of the gallows that would strangle the last vestage of life from the body of him who was ever kind to her and no matter what his faults or transgressions towards others were, he was always a kind brother to her, and spite of all efforts at self control her big, black eyes would fill with tears and flood out the awful vision.

Her father, less demonstrative, but none the less fully realizing the awful position in which his son was placed, made no sign, but sat most of the time with his head leaning wearily upon his hand, save when, from time to time, he was aroused by some strong point in the testimony of witnesses against his son, he would glance furtively with the sharp, penetrating gaze of his race at the witness, and after waiting to hear whether the lawyers could break the force of the evidence would sink back into his gulf of despair. Mike himself seemed as indifferent as when brought to this city by Captain Linden. He appeared to have a world of confidence in his own diagnosis of his case and never to have shaken off the idea that he was in no way connected with the murder because his companions did the shooting and carried away most of the money. It was only when he looked into the sorrowing eyes of his father that he seemed disconcerted by his surroundings. The eyes

that had cheered him on from the time when his infant feet first essayed the task of beginning life's journey were now sorrowing funeral lights in which every ray of brightness and hope had died out, and the glow he caught therefrom was only the flickering uncertain flame of the funeral pyre. He now looked into his father's eyes as if gazing into his own grave. It was a sad sight to see these three strangers in a strange land gazing vainly about for some friendly eye to look a kindness that they might not speak, but save the pitying glances of a few ladies who were present at the trial no reflex of hope or pity answered their appealing glances.

THE CASE OPENED.

Promptly at 9 o'clock the Judge entered, and the crier droned out the announcement that court was open.

The opposing attorneys took their seats and after a call of the jury list and the excusing of those not required in the case on trial, the case was opened by ex-District Attorney James Lenahan, who addressed the jury, stating what the Commonwealth expected to prove. He narrated in solemn and graphic language, the terrible events which took place on Oct. 19, 1888, declaring that outside of the defendant's own confession they expected to prove his guilty participation in the murder beyond a shadow of a doubt. In this case the State was demanding a human life in payment for two sacrificed, and would accept it only after the clearest proof. They would bring in evidence which would show that besides Mike there were two others taking part in the crime. These men, with the money, were now in Italy, but would at no distant day sit where Mike now sits, to answer for their part in the crime.

CHAPTER VIII.

TESTIMONY OF CHARLES MC'FADDEN.

HE first witness called was Charles McFadden. He is a railroad contractor. Knew and employed Bernard McClure for eight years as clerk and paymaster. McClure was 24 years old. He was single. His mother was a widow. After

beginning work on the mountain cut off, McClure was in the custom of drawing money from the Wyoming National Bank, taking it to the works and paying it out to the men. On the evening of Oct. 18, witness came from Philadelphia. The next morning he left Wilkes-Barre and drove out to the works. Met McClure and Flannaghan coming in. Went on to the works. About 10:30 left the works to return to Wilkes-Barre. When about a mile from the works, and at the top of the hill he saw the horse and wagon used by McClure standing in the road. He thought a runaway had occurred. Under the buggy were a blanket and robe. Got out, took hold of the robe and found McClure's body. Tied the horse to a stump and drove back to

JAMES L. LENAHAN.

Ex-District Attorney James L. Lennahan, under whose administration
the mountain murder was committed, and who ably as-
sisted in the conviction of "Mike."

the works. Gave the alarm and, taking Alex. McQuern with him, drove back. McQuern examined the body and McFadden looked at the horse. Saw that it was shot in the forehead and in the neck. They then drove on and found Flannagan's body. McQuern turned the body over and found that he was dead. Drove on to Miner's Mills and told of the murder. McQuern stopped there and, securing assistance, went back. McFadden came on to Wilkes-Barre and informed the officials. While driving out to the works witness saw two hunters with guns. Did not know them and never saw them again. The road is of nearly uniform grade, about 4 feet in 100. The distance between where McClure's body and Flannaghan's were found was about 1,500 feet. Witness was employing from 400 to 800 men. This was the last regular pay day. The men knew this, as many had been discharged on account of the finishing of the job.

Dr. Matlack, the next witness, is a practicing physician of Miner's Mills. Had known Bernard McClure for 15 years. On October 19, was told by Mr. McFadden that McClure had been killed. He drove to the spot and found his body lying in the road. Saw, also, Flannagan's body. Made only a cursory examination. Afterward was present at a postmortem examinatiom of McClure. Found two bullet wounds in his back, half an inch apart. The wounds ranged forward and upward. One bullet was lodged in the breast bone, another just under the skin. A bullet wound in the eye ranged upward and tore off the top of the skull. Any one of the shots would have proved fatal. Death must have resulted almost instantly.

CASHIER FLANAGAN TESTIFIES.

George H. Flanagan, sworn.—Am cashier of the Wyoming National Bank. Knew McClure. On Oct. 19, McClure took from the bank $12,000. The money had been put up the night before, in accordance with a memorandum furnished by McClure. Money was put up by Mr. Buckman, the teller of the bank. After putting up the money, of different denominations, the bills were put into a box and the coins into a canvas bag. Witness stayed to see this done, then put the two packages into the vault, locking it with a combination time lock. This could only be unlocked by himself at the proper time; next morning. On Oct. 19, about 9 o'clock McClure called for the money. Mr. Buckman, the teller, took the packages from the vault and gave them to McClure. These McClure put into a leather satchel.

Here witness was shown a good sized brown leather satchel of stout construction, but stained, weather beaten and covered with mildew, and having a cut the entire length of one side. Witness recognizes it by its peculiar make as like the one used by McClure, and unlike any other he had ever seen. Witness also recognized a bit of torn, soiled paper as the original memorandum, in McClure's handwriting, according to which the money had been put up. From this he read the list of the various denominations of bills and the amount of each. It agreed with a copy which had been made at the time by Mr. Buckman, and kept in the bank. A large canvass money bag, soiled and mildewed, was identified by witness as one of peculiar material, unlike any others used in the bank, and the one given to McClure on the day of the murder. Witness testified that the bank was accustomed to getting its small change from the other banks.

Mr. Mulligan, the teller of the Second National Bank, next sworn, was shown a small bag containing coin. He identified it as a package of quarters which he had put up and marked "$50." He believed the package had been delivered to the Wyoming National Bank.

Elmer Buckman sworn.—Am teller of Wyoming National Bank. I received a memorandum on Oct. 18, in McClure's handwriting, giving the denominations of money to be put for him. Witness identified the torn memorandum as the same. He put up the money in accordance with it. Identified the large canvas bag as one of peculiar make and material and similar to that given to McClure. The package of dimes was brought to the bank by George Miles. Recognized the leather satchel as McClure's.

George Miles, confectioner, sworn.—Frequently put up dimes in packages and deposited them at the Wyoming National Bank. Identified one of the soiled coin wrappers as having been used by him in putting up coin which was sent to the Wyoming National Bank.

As the weather beaten and mouldy valise, the torn and water-soaked wrappers, and the packages of small coin were brought to view, the excitement in the audience became intense. Here were mute but terrible witnesses against the prisoner. The insignificant and despised pennies and nickels, thrown aside by the murderers, now rising to condem them more strongly than could the larger sums in bil's and notes. The scene was highly dramatic.

AFTERNOON SESSION.

It was not half an hour after the close of the morning session, before the corridors of the Court House were jammed to suffocation

HENDRICK W. SEARCH.

HENDRICK W. SEARCH, Sheriff of Luzerne County, whose duty it will be to
execute Red Nosed Mike.

At 1:30 nine stalwart policemen entered the court room by the rear entrance, and marching to the upper end of the court room, opened a side door leading into the corridors, and began clearing the crowd out of the hallways. For half an hour they struggled and shouted, the mob shouting still louder, and for a time the task seemed hopeless. At 2 o'clock they had the building cleared, and formed a double line, between which a few at a time were permitted to enter and take seats. The first comers were a dozen or more well dressed women, who remained all through the session. There was even a greater rivalry than in the morning for seats inside the bar enclosure, many not entitled to seats forcing themselves in, to the inconvenience of lawyers and reporters. One well known dude, who had secured a seat in the morning, made himself conspicuously obnoxious by trying to drive out a gentleman who came earlier, and held the seat by both right and might. The crowd outside, not able to gain admittance, gathered about the windows. Soon they climbed upon the window ledge. The court crier closed the lower shutters. Then the eager sight-seekers stood up and looked over the blinds. The court finally ordered the upper blinds closed also. At a little after 2 o'clock the case was resumed.

Thomas F. Quigley, a merchant, and the postmaster of Miner's Mills was sworn. He testified to the events of the fatal morning. How Mike came to his store early in the day, visited the station, inquired concerning the trains, and left shortly before McClure arrived. Witness told of a conversation in his store in which Mike and a lot of other Italians had discussed the probable amount of each month's pay at the McFadden works. Some one had asked his opinion as to the probable amount and they had expressed a belief that it would be an easy matter to rob the paymaster.

A number of witnesses were called who had seen Mike near the scene of the murder about the time it occurred. Two witnesses saw also two Italians, one of whom carried an umbrella. Two hunters testified to passing along the road earlier in the day and meeting McFadden on the road. They left the road and went into the woods before the time of the murder.

One witness, H. W. Wilson, was in company with a Mr. Shepherd. They met first an unknown Italian, then two Americans, then two Italians. One hundred yards farther met Mike, and 175 yards farther McClure and Flannagan were met driving slowly up the mountain. Witness believed that one of the two Italians was the blacksmith, Bevevino.

John Lawler was at Mike's shanty about 12 o'clock on the day of the murder. Mike was behind a counter writing. Saw an Italian take a gun out and attempt to fire it. Could not, so Mike went out and discharged the gun. Mike then changed his shoes, stockings and pantaloons. Do not know why he did it.

William Oplinger, living at Parsons, testified next. In August, was in the woods near Laurel Run, hunting. Two Italians met him and wanted to look at his gun, which he permitted. The next day they and another Italian stopped at his house. They said they were going to Wilkes-Barre to buy a gun. One of the men was Mike. He told them to stop and show him the gun they bought, as they went home. They did so. He believed he would know the gun again if he were to see it.

Here Capt. Darte handed him an object on which all eyes were at once fastened with an intense interest. It was a rusted, weather beaten Winchester rifle. Witness took it carefully, being informed that it was loaded. He turned it over, threw it up to his shoulder, glanced along the barrel, set it down and declared that this was the gun. The defendant's attorneys attempted to shake his positive statement, but he declared stoutly that he was positive. He could tell it among a hundred of the same make and pattern.

Samuel Johnson, a neighbor of Oplinger, also saw the gun, and believe that this was the same one.

George Kemmerer, a clerk for T. C. Parker, of this city, testified to selling a rifle to Mike and another Italian for $18. They paid $15, and he trusted them to the balance, as he knew Mike through previous dealings. A few weeks later Mike brought the gun back, saying the owner was sick, and wanted his money refunded. This witness would not do, so Mike asked to leave the gun, to be sold, if possible, the money to be sent to an address in Philadelphia. In about two weeks Mike came in a third time and took the gun away again. This was about Sept. 1.

It was when Antonio Nopolello was called that excitement grew intense. He is the great "Unknown" whom Capt. Linden brought here early in January, and whom nobody had seen until now. He is a bright looking young fellow, about 19 years of age, and wonderfully quick of comprehension. At first it was thought that he would require an interpreter, but on trial he quickly dispelled any such misapprehensions. He testified that last July he worked for Col. Ricketts, near Laurel Run. Having a quarrel with one of the hands he left and went to Miner's Mills. Here he fell in with Mike, whom he asked to write a letter to his brother in Italy, for money, as he was out of that necessary article. When, after a long delay, an answer came saying his brother had no money, he was much disheartened. Mike was walking with him on the road to the postoffice, when Mike said: "Don't worry about that, I'll tell you something. You must not tell if I tell you. If you do I kill you, or my friends kill you." Then Mike said, "I want to kill the paymaster and get the money." I said, "No, Mike, I don't want to do anything like that. I wan't to live good in my heart, I never do such things." Then Mike again said, "If you tell what I have told you, you will be killed." Soon after he went with Mike and Bevevino to kill fish in the creek with dynamite. While there Bevevino told him they wanted to kill the paymaster. I said no, I have too much heart. He say, 'Oh, you got heart enough for 20 men. You better come on.' Then I say will not. I don't tell anybody what he told me because I am afraid and want get out best I can." Witness stayed around a few days longer, then went with Col. Ricketts' men to Shenandoah, on another job. When he left, he owed a woman $7, and she told him to pay it to Mike. He had never done so.

The cross examination of this witness was of great interest from its severity and from his ready wit, which enabled him to parry all attacks. He had first told Mike's proposal to him, about two weeks ago, when Capt. Linden's detective, Dimaio, came, was afraid to tell him at first, thinking he might be a friend of Mike, who was testing his fidelity in keeping the secret. When the detective said he was working for McFadden, witness told him.

"Why had you not told this before?"

"Because I afraid he friend of Mike, he kill me."

"Did he tell you what to testify?"

"No, he say, "You must tell the truth, nothing else."

"Why were you afraid Mike's friends would kill you? Is that the way Italians do?"

"Yes, that's way any peoples do to save the life."

"And you owed Mike $70?"

"No, no; not seventa dollars. Seven-a dollar. Five and two is seven, aint-a?"

Thomas Quigley, recalled, testified to a conversation he had with Mike, since Mike has been in jail. He asked Mike a number of questions concerning the murder, in which Mike acknowledged participation in it. Mike told him that he was going up the mountain when McClure and Flannagan passed him.

When he got to the place where Bevevino and Vellalli were concealed the shooting commenced. Bevevino shot McClure. Then Vellalli shot Flannagan. Mike fired from behind. Witness asked Mike if it was true that he was excited when he got to his shanty. Mike said, "No; I was cool as I am now."

THE MAN-MILLINER TESTIFIES.

Francisco Chiviacci, the cloak maker, is one of the most striking characters in the great trial. Of medium height—pale and thin featured—his blue eyes deep set and a fine nose with wide nostrils—his long wavy hair, light brown in color—neat attire and snowy collar—he seemed a picture of sensitive, fine feeling manhood. Graceful in every wave of his hand or bend of the head, his handsome light mustaches are frequently curled in a not overpleasant smile, which shows his handsome white teeth. Proud and fiery in disposition, the sarcastic manner and pointed questions of the cross-questioning attorney aroused his scornful anger, and he returned answers that lost none of their sharpness by the wonderful interpretation of Francis Dimaio, Jr., the handsome, dark featured Italian detective.

Dimaio, in turn, is nearly as remarkable in manner and appearance. The attorney for the defense puts a cutting question in sarcastic tones. The detective interpreter instantly translates it, preserving the very tones and manner of the lawyer. When the question is answered in melodious Italian, he as quickly gives its paraphrase in English, preserving, again, the witnesses' manner and tone. He evidences wonderful knowledge of what is or is not required, and he is a marvel of quickness and intelligence.

Mike, in turn, watches and listens to catch any error in interpretation, or variation in shade of meaning, and exhibits no small degree of intelligence, as he now asks for a different interpretation, or suggests question after question to his attorneys.

Chiviacci's testimony was that he had known Bevevino for six or seven years. That last November he first met Mike in Bevevino's company. The men were in Philadelphia

Afterwards Bevevino and Vellalli left on a steamer for Italy. Two days afterwards Mike came to him and inquired for Bevevino. Witness told him they had gone to Italy, but that Bevevino said he would send Mike a registered letter. Bevevino also left word for him to say to Mike, "I left because I saw the man with the big stomach." "I went there where he knows." "I did not see the young man." Mike seemed to feel bad and asked when the next steamer left for Italy.

CHAPTER IX.

MIKE'S TERRIBLE STORY.

Witness and Mike then took a walk around town. One Peirro's wife asked Mike if it was true that he had been arrested. Mike said yes, twice, but having been acquitted they could not try him again. They then went around to Capt. Linden's office. Mike said the Captain had twice saved him from death. Mike was sorry he had no money, since he always treated the Captain to good liquor and cigars. Witness asked Mike, "Is it true?" meaning about the arrest. Mike said yes. Witness told Mike "Bevevino told me," meaning that Bevevino told him. Mike had been chief officer of a secret society of Italians in Chicago. Mike thought this referred to the murder, and supposing witnesses knew the particulars, talked freely of his part in it. Mike boasted of his courage. Presently Mike began to talk and almost cried. Witness said, "You were not born to do a thing like this. From these tears you were dragged into it." No I was the instigator of the thing." Mike then went on to tell witness a wild story of the murder and of being in the woods three days and nights, part of the time he did not care for his victim. "You know how I used to drink beer! Now I do not care for it and cannot eat. A view comes of the man on the ground, the blood spurting from the mouth." Mike then boasted of Bevevino's courage, saying, "Why he was brave enough to shoot McClure in the mouth after he was dead." Witness asked how Mike dared call on Captain Linden, knowing he was connected with the police. Mike boasted that he was not afraid, saying, "See how calm I am now."

THE SECRET SOCIETY.

During Chiviacci's testimony it had been brought out that witness and Bevevino are from the same village in Italy and were former friends, witness sometimes calling Bevevino his god father. He explained that this was only a compliment, because of Bevevino's giving him a flower at the feast of St. John in May. The defense endeavored to draw out the fact that this giving of a flower was a sign of recognition of a secret society to which Chiviacci and Bevevino belonged, but this witness denied. It was evident, however, that there was more in this than he would admit. He declared that Bevevino and Mike belonged to such a society.

The defense endeavored to draw out from him just how he had been induced to make a statement to Capt. Linden, and although he admitted having been at Pinkerton head-

quarters several days and nights, the secret was not obtained. He declared positively that he did not know he had been indicted, or why he was held in jail. He had made no effort to find out.

THE CORONER'S TESTIMONY.

Coroner Mahon testified to the making of a post mortem examination of McClure and described the three wounds, any one of which, he said, would have caused death. He believed that the wound in the head was made with some blunt instrument, like the butt of a gun. He was shown the rifle and thought the stock of this was too thick to produce the narrow wound. (Dr. Matlack had testified that this wound was made by a bullet.) Darkness having settled upon the room at 5:45 p. m., the court adjourned until evening.

EVENING SESSION.

Long before the doors were opened in the evening the immense crowds embraced every available opportunity in order to gain admittance into the court room. At a quarter after seven the Judge took his seat and court was opened.

LINDEN ON THE STAND.

Capt. Linden said: "I live in Philadelphia. Am superintendent of the Pinkerton Detective Agency, of Philadelphia. The tracing of this crime was placed in my hands. I met Mike first in Philadelphia in November, in company with an Italian. He said 'He came to see his sister get mrrried.' I said nothing of the murder. He said 'he was going to Poughkeepsie afterwards. He thought McFadden might hurt him, that he had some grudge against him. He would show the people he was all right, that he did not commit the crime.' I next saw him January 3, at the Broad street station. I took him to my office. I told him I had arrested him for the murder of McClure and Flannagan. Told him he need not say anything of the crime unless he wanted to. He said 'he was innocent.' I told him I wanted what money ho had. If he could not give me some of the stolen money I did not want any. I then left him to get supper. After I came back I asked him if he had reflected over what I had told him. I again told him he need not say one word about the crime unless he was so disposed. He then looked about the room and said, 'Is anybody here?' I looked to see. Thayer had been there previously. I said to Mike there is nobody here but you and I, and God above us. He then said, 'I will tell you all.' I did not arrest him until he sat down in my office. I then told him I knew all about this case and said, 'if you lie to me I will know it. I never mentioned the word hang to Mike. I never said to him you had better tell all.

"Did you hold out any inducement to him?" asked the attorney.

"I did not—no, never."

"Did you instruct Thayer, your detective, to make any offer or inducement to him?"

"No, sir. I told Thayer to take Mike up stairs and be careful to make no promises or threats of any kind, but if he said anything to make a note of what he said. I was particularly careful not to hold out any inducements to him."

"Did you not say to him that if he would tell the truth you would see that he would come out all right?"

"I never used such language. But afterwards, at the time he showed me the articles on the mountain, I said, 'It is clear, Mike, you have done right.' "

DETECTIVE THAYER'S STORY.

At this point Frank Thayer was called to the stand. He said: "I know the defendant. On the 3d of January I met him in Philadelphia in Captain Linden's office. He was with an Italian. I was not instructed by Linden to make any offers to Mike of clemency. I made no such offers to him. I only said he had better tell the Captain all he knew of the affair. I said: "Mike if I were in your place I would tell all I knew. It will be better for you in the end. I never said

anything about escaping the penalty of the law by turning State's evidence. I have been a detective for several years. I have told you all I said to Mike by the way of promise. I said the Captain will take care of you while you are here. I said nothing to Mike about this country regarding crimes.

MIKE ON THE STAND.

"When you were in Philadelphia in January, in Linden's office, who did you go there with?" asked the defense.

"With the Captain. When I was in the office he told me to sit down. He then said, 'Mike, I am sorry, but I have a warrant for you. It is too bad. I had to get it. I got it from Wilkes-Barre I must arrest you.' He asked me how much money I had. I told him not much. Captain asked me how much money I spent in Poughkeepsie. I said not very much. He told me to tell all I knew. He told me he had all the evidence about me. I said all right then, if you got it you don't want it from me. I said, I will tell you the truth. He took me on the second floor, where there were three other young men. He told the officers there to give me anything I wanted. He then went out. In about five minutes Thayer came in. He shook hands with me. He took me in another room. He asked me if I told anything to the Captain yet. I said no. He said Captain Linden had discharged him because he had had a little trouble with him. He then said, 'Mike, the best thing you can do is to tell the Captain everything.' I said I did not know anything. He said the law of this country is that if a man makes a confession or statement he will not get hung. He may get a few years in prison. He said: 'You had better tell Captain all.' Then he said: 'Mike, I have always been a friend of yours.' I said again, 'Frank I do not know anything.' He said: 'At any rate you tell what you know to the Captain and you will come out all right.' We then went donw stairs. I asked Thayer if the Captain was in the office. He telephoned to the Captain and said: 'Mike wants to see you.' I said I want to see the Captain alone. The Captain then came in. We both sat down. He said, 'Now Mike, you don't need to say anything if you don't want to. He then mentioned the names of Bevevino and Vellalli, and how they were concerned. He then said, 'I have evidence to arrest you, Mike, in the name of God tell me the truth.' I said. Captain, I do not know anything. He said, 'I have defended you before, I will defend you still. Tell me all you know and I will see that you come out all right." I then told him to get a sheet of paper. Here the witness was dismissed for the time.

LINDEN RECALLED.

I instructed Thayer not to hold out any promisees to Mike while he was in his custody. Before Mike made the coufession I asked him whether or not he had reflected on the subject. He said, "I have nothing to say." He sat still for awhile. He then said, "Captain, is anybody here?" I then went to see whether we were alone. I said to him, "There is nobody here but you and I and the God above us." I knew he was about to say something. I said, "If you have anything to say tell me nothing but the truth. I will make you no promises of getting off, but anything you say I will use against you. But if you say anything, tell me the whole of God's truth."

At this point the defense objected to the admission of the confession. Attorney Garman said that the statements of Linden, Thayer and Mike show that what was promised by Thayer to Mike was said in order to get something out of him. "It is improper to admit the confession because of the promises held out to Mike by Thayer as an employe of Linden, which fact Mike knew. We think the confession should not be admitted in evidence. It is clear that Linden expected a confession when Mike came out of the private room with Thayer. The expression of Thayer that the Captain would take care of him induced the belief that the Captain would take care of him in shielding him from punishment if he made a confession; that the law would not hang him but might put him in prison for a few years." Several authorities were cited, showing that confessions made under such circumstances are inadmissable. "It is now agreed that any promises held out that it would be better in the end to make a coufession vitiates it."

Attorney John T. Lenahan, for the prosecution, thought that if Capt. Linden were taken from the case and the prisoner would have been put in Thayer's custody for good, the position would be different. But here Linden is in the case and tells the prisoner that he need not say anything if he did not wish to; that Thayer here had no authority to make promises while under the superior from whom he received instructions not to hold forth hope of reward or promises of clemency in order to extract a confession. There might be some color to the position of the defense if Thayer had remained in the room; but he went out, and before he left Linden cautioned Mike not to say anything unless he wented to. Thus Mike knew Linden's intention before he went into the room with Thayer.

Mr. Garman thought the evidence of Capt.

Linden alone would be strong enough to throw out the confession because he spoke such things as: "We will take care of you," etc., although they might not have meant it as Mike understood it. The mind of the prisoner was confused, and he knew not how to construe the words. Mike understood Linden to say that he would be entirely protected if the confession was made.

The court said that there was no doubt that if Thayer was an officer, having custody of the prisoner, and the language of Thayer was such as to hold forth promise from Linden, the case would be different. Was it the inducement from the Captain, and did the defendant suppose there was that authority in Thayer to speak for Linden? Thayer himself said to Mike that he was discharged. Mike did not suppose that Thayer was speaking for his superior officer on account of this. The promise must be the inducement for the confession in order to vitiate it; but if the inducement is not there, then the confession is voluntary. According to the testimony of Captain Linden, Mike was told that he would receive no promise, and all he said would be used against him. This, of itself, would show that Thayer had no authority in holding out any promises. We think the confession should, under all the circumstances, be received. The objection is overruled, confession admitted, and bill sealed for the defendant.

Captain Linden was then told to say all Mike had told him after he had told Mike he need not say anything.

Here Captain Linden told an oral confession which Mike had told him in the office when he asked him the above question. The same story was the next day taken down by Linden's stenographer. The confession was signed in Wilkes-Barre the following day. (We refrain from publishing this confession here for the reason that Mike tells the story all over again while on the witness stand in his own defence.)

Linden then said: "We left Philadelphia, I, Thayer and Mike. We arrived in Wilkes-Barre. We wanted to see if Mike told the truth about where the money was. We were too late for the train. We then decided to walk to Parsons. I sent Thayer into a store to get a lamp. He brought one. We then walked to the upper end of the town. Then went on, Thayer in the lead, up the hill. Mike was in the middle. He directed the way when we reached the woods. We walked in Indian file. We at length came to two trees. Mike spied one of them which he had marked. I then lit the lamp. Mike pointed to the place where the gun was. He took away the stones and took out the gun. Thayer examined it. I then asked where the money was. There were also about 18 cartridges in the same hole. Mike then went a few feet from there and, diving in with his hand, brought out a tin can. He reached down again and brought up a large bag. (Here the articles were produced in court.) There was a little over $18 in the can. I opened the bag and saw there was money there. Tied it up and put it back. We went further down. Thayer held the light. Mike hunted in two places and at last found the satchel, frozen in the ground. It took all his strength to pull it out. He first pulled out the gun cover. Before he took the gun out he took the halter strap out and holding it up, said, 'There is where Bevevino cut it.' He then took the satchel out and said, 'There is where Bevevino cut it open.' He said he took the money out. I told him to put the things back. I took the money. We went back to Wilkes-Barre in another direction. When we came to the railroad, I cut the letter V on the end of a tie and told Thayer of it in order to locate the spot for further use. Our lamp then went out. Mike carried the bag nearly all the way. He would not give it up. He said, "I am strong." When we found the money Mike said. "There, now you will believe me." I said, "Yes; you have done right." At ten minutes of two we went into Lohmann's and took breakfast. We counted the money. There was $251.59. We went to the Exchange Hotel. In the afternoon I took Mike to Squire Rooney's and waived a hearing. I took the money to the Wyoming Bank, gave it to Mr. Flanagan and took his receipt. I took Mike to jail. The same day, on the morning of the 5th, I sent Thayer with County Detective Heffernan to go to the mountain and get the articles and take them to the Wyoming Bank and leave them there. Before he had left the Exchange Hotel, the confession was signed by Mike in the presence of the witnesses."

It was here developed that Mike had not read all of the confession brought into court before he signed it and the defense objected to its admission. Only part of the paper had been read to Mike.

The judge overruled the objection, because Mike knew what it contained. The confession was admitted.

CHAPTER X.

PROBABLY no document ever before read in the courts of this State was listened to with closer or more profound attention than was given to the reading of Mike's confession to Captain Linden by counsel for the prosecution, John T. Lennahan. The interest was more than doubled by the belief that the confession to Linden would differ materially from that already published as coming from Mike through Postmaster Quigley. There was no such difference. The main points of the story were substantially covered in the Quigley confession and a big sigh of relief seemed to escape from the assembled multitude as it realized that the connection of Mike with the crime still rested on the well defined lines as exposed from time to time by Mike's own story and by all subsequent development of surrounding circumstances. As Counsular Lennahan closed the reading Judge Rice adjourned court until the following day.

. THIRD DAY'S PROCEEDINGS.

The general interest had subsided somewhat after the public had assured itself that Mike's counsel had no surprises to offer in rebuttal of the awful testimony furnished by his own confession.

Captain Linden was recalled to testify as to some of the detective work. When asked what brought Mike from Poughkeepsie, witness answered that one of the detectives had written a letter to Mike's companion, De Luska, purporting to come from his father, and another apparently from his lawyer. De Luska inveigled Mike into the trip on the strength of these letters.

No one on the Pinkerton force but Capt. Linden, and no one else knew that De Luska, or Dimaio, as he is rightly called, was a member of the force. Dimaio came to Philadelphia with Rezzolo; he was attired in an old fur cap, a rough red woolen shirt, a pair of ragged trousers and rough boots. "He was a tough looking customer, and I wouldn't have known him if he hadn't been with Rezzolo," said the witness, smiling grimly. The agency at Philadelphia occupies four stories of a five story building. The detectives of the force are known at the office by number and not by name. Witness described how Dimaio was arrested in good faith by one of the detectives, who did not know him. He then told of inviting Rezzolo to his office, telling him, "I have something to show you—something that will take a load off you." At the office, after telling Rezzolo he knew all about the murder, he advised him to tell all. He then left Rezzolo in charge of Thayer, who was writing it down. Then sent for a short hand reporter and took down the full confession, which had been read in court.

Frank Thayer, a detective, 27 years of age, married, was next on the stand, and told of the trip with Rezzolo and Capt. Linden to the spot where the money had been buried. The night was very dark. Witness walked ahead in the narrow path through the woods. Rezzolo walked next, then Capt. Linden. Witness was watching Rezzolo closely, as he was not handcuffed. When they got to the place and Rezzolo dug up the rifle, witness feared it was loaded and took it out of his hands. Witness identified the numerous articles as the ones found. Ex-County Detective Heffernan and Supt. Alex. Mitchell testified to being present next day when Thayer removed the articles. This closed the evidence for the prosecution.

EVIDENCE IN DEFENSE.

Salvator Rezzalo, a dark faced Italian with long scanty locks, a short, black beard, coarse woolen shirt and rough suit, was the first witness in defense. Through the interpreter he testified that he was the father of Mike. That he came to Wilkes-Barre on Thursday in answer to a telegram. Mike's mother was sick. Mike is 19 years old.

MIKE ON THE STAND.

Michael Rezzolo, or "Red Nosed Mike," now took the stand, and talked steadily for over two hours. He was allowed to testify without any interruption, and while he never deviated from the exact line of his story, he went into every minute and trivial detail. Slowly and delibeartely, he spoke with all the steadiness of clockwork. At first every listener leaned forward and gave breathless attention to his words. Then as it was seen that much of the story was uninteresting they leaned back and only showed close attention when the witness was talking directly of the plot, the purchase of the rifle, or comission of the murder. Mike began by stating that he came to Wilkes-Barre on Jan. 18, 1888. He told of his work here, of his keeping a small commissary store, of his acquaintance with archfiend Bevevino. Bevevino was soon discharged, and witness told how he lay about the works idle and desolate. Then came the story of the first mention of the plot how, after a walk in the woods with Bevevino

and Nappolelo, they practiced shooting with their revolvers. How Bevevino boasted. "How we three fellows could fight if somebody came along." This murderous idea seemed to have orignated at the smell of powder and it was followed by the first suggestion of robbing the paymaster.

"Then Bevevino said how Flannaghan and McClure walk lone through the woods. They walk slow—easy to make money. Then he look at me and Antonio (Nappelelo) Then he say, 'You like to do that?' I say, You bet." He next told of Nappolelo's need of money and failure to get any from home. Of his discouragement, and being out of work. One day Bevevino took Nappolelo about thirty yards from the shanty and talked for ten minutes. When they came back, witness asked Nappolelo what they were talking of. Nappolelo said of the paymaster, and asked Mike 'What do you say." Rezzolo replied, "I say whatever you say?". Nappolelo then said, "I am not satisfied to do it, Rezzolo answered "All right." Bevevino chided them for their want of courage. A few days later Rezzolo and Bevevino came to town and bought the rifle of T. C. Parker. On the way home Bevevino talked of nothing but the secret society he belonged to, and of his great courage—how he had taken part in many robberies. I told him, "sometime you hang, try talk of something else." Bevevino persisted, saying he had been there before. Had done such work in Italy.

MIKE'S FEAR OF BEVEVINO.

"Until that time, I not afraid of Bevevino. He said he could do the job alone, but better, two more men with him. Said me and Nappolelo could do it. I said, Nappolelc does not want to, and I have not the courage. He said, 'Mike, if you don't want to you need not, but you must look out for my friends.' I said, I have as many friends as you. He said his friends were different—belonged to secret society."

On arriving near the cabin, the rifle was hidden. A few weeks later, during Bevevino's absence in Philadelphia, Mike went and got the rifle, took it back to Captain Parker, and asked him to sell it and send the money to Bevevino. Mike tells that not long afterwards, for fear of Bevevino, he left here, went to Newark, where he worked for a time as a barber. He was afterwards persuaded to return to the works. When he returned, Bevevino was angry at not finding the rifle, and Rezzolo on his return was compelled to go to Parker's, this time, Bevevino came with him, also an Italian named Villalli. On their way home Bevevino began talking of the murder, when Rezzolo told him to "shut up," fearing Villalli. Bevevino then informed him that Villalli was in the plot. Two days before the murder. Bevevino asked if he was not satisfied to take a part. Rezzolo said no. Bevevino replied, "This thing got to be done. I have friends to do the shooting. We don't need you. If we need you, you can shoot. If any man loses his courage, he will be punished right there. You must let us know when they are coming."

THE FATAL DAY.

Rezzolo declares that the talk on Oct. 17 was his last conversation with Bevevino. On the morning of the 19th business called him to McFadden's headquarters. He went there early in the morning, then to his mother's shanty, where his mother was in bed sick. He shook hands and said good bye, then went to Miner's Mills.

Up to this point, Rezzolo had told his story with great minuteness of detail. Now his expression became more rapid. He seemed intensely excited, and hurried from one important event on the morning to another with nervous haste. Words would not come fast enough, and his voice grew hoarse. The excitement in the audience was fearful, everyone leaning forward with eyes fixed upon the prisoner, and ears strained to catch the awful words. Many in the room were greatly moved by the tragic story.

TELLS HOW THE DEED WAS DONE.

"I got to Miner's Mills at 8 o'clock. I went to depot to see about train—I stay at Quigley's little while and get my mail. A man with long whiskers was there—and we drank together—stayed there till 10 minutes of 10, then go towards shanty. I met three men —Then I met Wilson and Frenchy—When I

get White House road—I don't know anything—I don't know McClure and Flannaghan down—I don't know they went for money—The men not tell—me they do this thing. When I get to White House road—they passed me—The old man he spoke to me. The buggy go lively. When they get about seventy feet away. I had an umbrella in my hand. I see Bevevino come out of brush and shoot McClure. (Sob.) Twice, I think. McClure sit on right side. After Bevevino shot McClure he shoot other man, two or three times. (Sobs.) Then Flannagan fall out. After he shoot Flannaghan, Bevevino look at me and curse me. Not point rifle at me. He say Jesus Christ hurry up! Bevevino look very white. I get scared from way he spoke, three or four days before, about men lose courage. That's what makes me pull out revolver, shoot three or four times. When Bevevino shoot, Villalli shoot, then run away. All time horse run away—Bevevino run after, look back, say nothing. He catch horse, shoot him lots of times. After he shoot— horse—he shoot—McClure—in—the—head— after— he—is — dead —then—he—told—me— (These last words were uttered in a horse whisper, and the prisoner broke down and sobbed convulsively. (It was several minutes before he could continue and the audience sat in painful, breathless silence) told me to take the gun and shoot any one who comes."

A few words told of Bevevino's cutting the strap, securing the valise, and their flight through the woods near Mike's shanty, where they hid money and gun. At this point Judge Rice adjourned court with startling suddenness, to resume at 2 p. m.

CHAPTER XI.

AFTERNOON SESSION.

It soon got noised abroad that Mike was on the stand telling his story and the most tremendous crowd since the opening of the trial gathered in the corridors as the time for court to reassemble approached. The police had the utmost difficulty in keeping order. It was 2.15 before the Judge gave the order for the trial to proceed and Mike once more took the stand. He then continued his testimony as follows:

"When we got back to the shanty the people were drinking beer; I changed my clothes for my pants were very wet; after I put on dry clothes I saw there was no bread there so I took a bag and went to Frank's shanty to get some; near Frank's shanty I

met Bevevino; he asked me why I was there and I told him; then I went down to my father's shanty to get some bread; Bevevino followed me; met a man who spoke about the murder. Bevevino told me not to be afraid to keep up my courage. At my father's I saw Robert Petrello; he was talking about the murder; my father had no bread and we went back to my shanty. Pretty soon an engine came up the road; there was O'Brien, Heffernan and others on it; I gave them something to drink; they then said: 'Mike, we'd like to see you.' They told me that McFadden had sent them up and he wanted to see me at Quigley's. Then O'Brien said, 'We want to find out about the men who have been away from the works. If you don't help

us we'll arrest you for selling beer without a
licence.' I said I would help them all I could.
We went to my father's shanty and called
Petrello. Then we went to the shanties to
find out who had been away, but could not
find anything particular. Joseph Pierro was
at my shanty that evening. He asked me
where Bevevino was that morning and I said
'At home.' Then he said that Bevevino was a
very bad man. That night we went down to
Miner's Mills and we found Quigley's store
crowded with people. Quigley asked me
where I had been that morning and I told
him the story I had thought of. Bevevino
and I went to the money the second day after
the shooting and took some of the money. I
got about $160 altogether from that money.
The second time we went to the money Bevevino gave me two $50 bills. Then when
Bevevino and Vellalli came to Poughkeepsie
they gave me $50. They stayed a few days
and then went to Philadelphia. I have not
seen them since.

"I first got acquainted with De Luska at
Poughkeepsie when he came there to the
works. He came to our shanty quite frequently and we became acquainted. He
seemed to be different from what the other
men were. He spoke better and was not like
them. One day McFadden's superintendent
asked me if I knew any one who would do
for book-keeper or time-keeper. I told him
about De Luska, and McFadden engaged him.
After that De Luska was always very friendly.
Some time after that he told me his father was
in Wilmington and he would like to take me
there. He offered to pay my fare, but at first
I would not go. Finally, however, I said I
would go, and we went together from Poughkeepsie to Philadelphia. When he got off the
train he told me to wait a moment and went
away. Then Capt. Linden came up and asked
me how I came there. I told him I came
with a friend. The Captain said, 'Where is
he?' I pointed to De Luska and said, 'There.'
Then Dougherty and Linden got hold of him
and he said to me, 'Mike, have you brought
us to Philadelphia to be arrested?' I had to
explain to Captain Linden, but he said,
'Mike, never mind him, he's all right.' Then
the Captain and I went down to his office."

Mike then gave a detailed statement of
what was said between them in the office that
night, before he made the confession.

After he had been taken to the office and
arrested he was given into charge of Thayer.
Concerning this the witness testified as follows:

"Thayer told me to tell everything I knew
to the Captain and he would treat me to anything. He asked me where the things were
hid. He said, 'You tell me where they are
hid; I will go and take them away where no
one can find them,' I told him I knew nothing about it. He said again that it would be

better for me to tell all I knew, for in this
country when any man makes a statement of
that kind he got off clear. I told him again
that I knew nothing about it. Then we went
down to Captain Linden's office and we sat
there together. Thayer went away. The
Captain asked me to tell all I knew. He said:
'Mike, I helped you before. You have got
lots of life about you. You don't want to
sacrifice your life for others.' I told him
again that I knew nothing about it. He spoke
to me again and promised in the name of God
to help me if I would tell, and then I told
him to get a sheet of paper and I told all.

"At the shooting I did not fire at the men.
I fired my pistol into the ground."

Mr. Garman—Why did you not run away
when you saw Bevevino come out of the
bushes and shoot?

Mike—Because of Bevevino had said to me
before, that he would kill any one who lost
heir courage.

"Did you know Bevevino and Vellalli were
going to be there?"

"No, sir."

"Did you come down to Quigley's and go
up that road in accordance with any plan
with Bevevino and Vellalli?"

"No, sir; I did not."

"Why did you not tell some one about
what Bevevino proposed to do?"

"I dare not because of what he had told
me. He told me what he was and all the robberies he had done in Italy. If he was in the
country yet I would never have said a word
about it. I thought he had more friends in
this matter than he had."

"Did you shoot at McClure or Flanigan that
day?"

"No, sir. I fired off my revolver in the
ground. Bevevino cursed me and told me to
hurry up. He had the rifle in his hands and
turned towards me, and then I fired my revolver."

"What led you to make this statement to
Captain Linden?"

"The way they talked to me. I believed
they would protect me. He helped me before
and I believed that he would do so again."

John T. Lenahan then put the defendant
through a severe cross-examination. Mike
admitted that he knew McClure well and
that McClure was very kind to him and
helped him along. Antonio Napolelo had refused from the first to have anything to do
with the murder; Mike never told McClure
about the scheme to murder him, nor sent
him any word by mail or any other way. Mr.
Lenahan:

"How many times did you and Bevevino
visit the place where the money was hid before you killed McClure?"

"In the name of God I never killed Mo-
Clure," burst out the prisoner.

"Oh, I won't hurt your feelings; I take it

back; we will say, 'before McClure died,'" said Lenahan.

"What brought you to Philadelphia the first time?"

"I went to see some friends. A cousin of mine had his family there."

"Why did you go to Chiviacco?"

"I went to find out about Bevevino and Vellalli.

"They had gone to Italy?"

"Yes sir."

"What did you want with Bevevino and Vellalli?"

"I wanted to see them."

"What for?"

"Oh, I just want to see them. To speak to them."

"They had the money with them in Philadelphia, had they not?"

"Yes, sir."

"Did you not go there to meet them and get your share?"

"No, sir; I did not."

"Did not Bevevino arrange to send money to you through Chiviacco?"

"That's what Chiviacco says."

"Did you send a letter to Bevevino through Chiviacco, asking him for money?"

"I sent a letter to Chiviacco to send to Bevevino, asking for some money, so I could give it to this man if he said anything."

"Did you not say in your letter to Chiviacco that the blacksmith had not treated you right?"

"I may have done."

"You wrote to Bevevino through Chiviacco frequently and received replies in the same way, did you not?"

"Yes, I did."

"Why did you fire your pistol on that road?"

"Because Bevevino scared me. He cursed me and told me to hurry up."

"Why did you not run away?"

"How could I run?"

"Did not Vellalli run?,'

"Yes."

"Then why could not you?"

"Because I dare not."

In following up the cross-examination Mr. Lenahan called Mike down from the stand and made him illustrate the relative positions of Bevevino and McClure when the shooting took place.

"Then Bevevino was at the side of McClure?"

"Yes, sir."

"And Vellalli was in front, someway up the road?"

"Yes, sir."

"And you were behind them?"

"Yes, sir."

"Then was it not you, sir, that fired those slugs into McClure's back?"

"No, sir, it was not."

"How could Bevevino fire those shots from where he was?"

"I don't know."

Mr. Lynch—Did you shoot either of these men?

"No, sir, and did not intend to, either."

"Did you shoot that horse?"

"No, sir, I shot nothing."

After a good deal more examination and cross-examination the defendant left the stand.

BURGESS MOOR AGAIN.

The defense then called Burgess Moore, of Miner's Mills, to the stand again who testified that Bevevino was present at the hearing given Mike before the witness. Bevevino was so seated that he could see Mike and hear all he said.

This closed the evidence for the defense. The prosecution offered nothing in rebuttal and Judge Rice announced the evidence closed and the witnesses discharged.

After a brief consultation among the attorneys court adjourned until 7:15 P. M.

SATURDAY EVENING SESSION.

As the great trial was nearing its close, and it became known that John T. Lenahan, the celebrated criminal lawyer, would speak for the people against the murderer, the rush for places was more pronounced than ever, and many stood for hours outside the Court House, vainly hoping to hear some of the burning words of the able lawyer.

Judge Rice and the jury took their seats at about 7 o'clock, and after order was obtained, Mr. Lenahan began one of the most impressive pleas ever heard in Luzerne County Courts. The following is a brief condensation of the main features of the address:

"If ever a murder of first degree was made out it is in this case. I approach this summing up with fear and trembling lest some of the many points be forgotten. This murderer laid in wait, he deliberated, he premeditated and he committed. Months and months were devoted to the consummation of the crime. When Bernard McClure, in the nobleness of his heart, befriended this man who sits at this defendant's table, this man premeditated murder most foul. We as an American nation extended this man the freedom and liberty of this country. He repaid us with crime most foul. Of all diabolical crimes this was the worst. We often hear of men in the heat of passion, striking down a foe, but how seldom do we hear of three men, strangers to our shores, participating in such a sober deliberate crime?

"The two men who were victims of this cruel crime, were seen in our fair city, seen at Miner's Mills, and then were no more. In the full bloom of health, in the possession of a happy home, they were struck down. And on the scene of the crime appeared a man who swore that, if necessary, the fortune of forty years' hard work would be spent in bringing to justice the perpetrators of the crime. Contractor McFadden loved Bernard McClure as he loved a son; he loved Hugh Flannigan as he loved a father. The Pinkertons were employed. They are tireless and never sleep, and soon the leader in this crime was in the hands of the law. He makes a confession to Captain Linden. He makes a confession to Thomas Quigley. Like all criminals, when conquered, he was prepared to make terms. These terms:

"Sold his conspirators into the hands of the law. When this arch criminal approached young Nappolelo, who was supposed to be ready for crime, and suggested this crime, the young man in honor refused. The man, who was *led into the crime*, laid in wait two days and two nights—on one of them the rain was pouring in torrents—for the blood of Bernard McClure. This is the man, gentlemen who is such an innocent. For two days Bernard McClure and Hugh Flanigan did not dream that the angel of death was hovering around their heads. On that dreary, stormy morning, this blood-thirsty Italian laid in wait for the heart's blood of his friends. Oh, is he not guilty? One fact alone is sufficient to prove his guilt—the fact that he was there. You saw, gentlemen, how the tears came to his eyes, bidden or unbidden, when he told how Bevevino came up to that dead man and put a bullet into that cold brain.

"We ask not, gentlemen of the jury, that you bring in a verdict of murder in the first degree if the evidence don't warrant it. Did you notice how coolly and callously he told that story of murder and bloodshed? It made my blood run cold to hear this red-handed villain tell how the murder was done. For days these men looked for a suitable spot to dip their hands in the blood of their fellow men. Month after month this man watched the visits of McClure with the coming of pay day. In his confession he says, 'I came along the road the morning of the murder. I passed two wagons and a number of Italians. I did not speak.' No, he did not speak. He had other designs. When he looked upon them again it was with death in his eye.

"Why did that man go out on that dump on that morning? Why, gentlemen, it was to look down with his eagle eye over the highway and see if that satchel was in the wagon, for that satchel was only used when it was filled with money. Like a sleuth hound then does he follow these men and soon this thug and member of the Mafia is reeking with blood.

"Gentlemen of the jury, send in a verdict such as will teach these foreign vagabonds and murderers that crime cannot be committed with impunity."

During this grand piece of oratory Mike sat and eyed the speaker without any visible sign of emotion.

THE DEFENSE.

E. A. Lynch, counsel for the defence, began his address by quoting from the Constitution of State, the clause, according to which everyone charged with a crime such as this, is entitled to a fair and public trial, by a jury of his peers, according to the law and the evidence, uninfluenced by public clamor. He said that it was in obedience to that wise and human provision that he and his colleague were there to offer such a defense as the nature of the case allowed. It was not a voluntary act of theirs. They were simply acting as part of the machinery of the court, in order that justice might be done under the Constitution.

He said that within the walls of this temple of justice were not only the ordinary penny-a-liners of the press, who daily howl for the blood of the poor, friendless Italian, but scribes who have the audacity to prejudice the case in their editorial columns before either the judge or jury could form any legal conclusion as to the guilt or innocence of the prisoner at the bar.

He referred to the force arraigned against the defendant, namely, the oldest detective agency of the United States, backed by the wealth of the State, and supported by one of the ablest district attorneys who ever sat at the prosecutor's table. His eloquent successor, and last, but not least, the flower of Luzerne bar, John T. Lenahan, while on the other side, a poor Italian, friendless and alone, with two attorneys assigned him by the court, without any opportunity to master the facts of the case from the defendant's standpoint.

He dwelt upon the excellent character borne by the defendant since his arrival in this country. He was liked and trusted by all. He claimed that the theory of the prosecution that Mike was the arch conspirator in this foul crime was false, but that the evidence showed that Guissippi Bevevino was the master mind that plotted the murder, and that Michael Rezzolo was so completely under his influence that he was not a free agent. That he was in such mortal terror of his life at the hands of Bevevino and the society of assassins to which he belonged, that there was nothing left for him but to obey. He made an eloquent and forcible plea for his client, and certainly made the best of a very bad bargain.

At the conclusion of Mr. Lynch's argument Judge Rice sopke as follows:

GENTLEMEN OF THE JURY—I am very sorry that we shall not be able to finish the case to-night. The defendant's counsel have very little time in preparation. I think it is our duty to dispose of the case deliberately and not limit counsel in their argument. We will hold you until Monday morning. We suggest, as we did before, that you wait until the case is finally concluded before entering into any discussion which would prejudice your minds one way or the other, and with extreme caution not to have any communication with any person out of the court, upon any subject. Of course, the officers will make you as comfortable as possible to-morrow, and we hope on Monday morning you will be refreshed from the arduous labors of the week and at that time the case will be concluded. The prisoner is remanded."

The crier then formally announced the adjournment of court until Monday morning.

The great murder trial was the chief topic of conversation throughout the city all day Sunday, and wherever men met there was sure to be heard the question: "What do you think will be the outcome of the great trial?" Some wisely shook their heads, and desiring to be on the safe side declined to express any opinion. Many others boldly stated that if the past history of Luzerne County juries was to be taken as a criterion in the present case, there was lots of room for doubt as to what conclusion the jury would arrive at. The evidence, the make-up and character of the jury and jurymen, were all taken into consideration with a freedom that is seldom heard in murder trials, and it can be truthfully said that there was but one ending to all controversies in connection with the case and that was that knave or fool the Italian Rezzolo deserved the halter.

Court convened promptly at the hour of 9 o'clock on Monday morning, and the

FOURTH DAY OF THE TRIAL

had began to make its record. Court Crier Barnes announced the fact, the jury was polled and the prisoner again looked upon the faces of the men who held his life in their hands. They are fair men, good men, and as intelligent as God ever made, and herein lay Rezzolo's greatest danger.

They are men of high character and good citizens, who, having a duty to perform, will not shrink through sickly sentimentalism from performing that duty. Rezzolo reads this in their solemn eyes, and beneath the contact of their looks his own dim with the all-too-late tears of contrition, fully realizing the awful truth that to him "who showeth mercy, mercy will be shown."

His counsel, John A. Garman, also has a duty to perform. Under instructions from the Court he must do the best he can for his client; in other words he must make the best of a bad job. But he does nobly under the circumstances when he pleads the great fear his client had for the Italian Maifa Chief, Bevevino, he reaches a climax worthy a better cause. Continuing, he said substantially:

If the jury believed that he was in fear of his life, and that his presence on the fatal spot was an unfortunate circumstance, they could not find him guilty of murder in the first degree. The witnesses against Mike were sharply criticised. Chiviacci was referred to

as "the sneaking, snarling traitor who, in the name of friendship—the worthy god-son of a worthy god-father—a man who told with a snarling smile everything that went against Mike, and whose lips were scaled when asked any question which would tell against his friend Bevevino."

The unseemly haste, as it was termed, with which the case had been pushed was accounted for by the eagerness of the Pinkerton agency to find a victim. They had found that the real perpetrators had escaped them and they brought all their forces to bear upon the defendant. The speaker detailed the circumstances occurring before the murder and endeavored to show that they were not in themselves suspicious. The terrors of the Italian vendetta were pictured in graphic words, and the devilish persistency of Bevevino, in constantly referring to the proposed murder, thus poisoning the minds of the two boys, Nappolello and Mike, was made much of. The fact that Mike, the alleged principal, remained penniless in this country, while his assistants in crime escaped with $12,000, was pointed out as showing the inconsistency of the prosecution. The attorney made a plausible argument to show that since the purpose of the law was to correct the criminal and protect society, the verdict of murder in the second degree, with a penalty of 24 years, would be sufficient to satisfy justice.

The prisioner, during his lawyer's able plea, had watched him with breathless interest, his face flushing and growing pale by turns. As the lawyer approached the subject of the killing, and described Bevevino's devilish conduct during the killing. Mike's face flushed, his eyes filled with tears, and he hung his head and cried bitterly, though without covering his face.

The only brief hope he had enjoyed during the whole trial had opened the flood gates of his soul, and guilty and all as he was and is, his heart went out in gratitude even toward the man, who, in charge of public duty, found some excuse for his client's awful part in the bloody deed. But the culprit's joy was of short duration; for a moment later another pleader stood up and began the presentation of the victims' side of the case, and hope died out of his eyes.

DISTRICT ATTORNEY DARTE

began in slow and measured terms his address, in which he pictured the ruthless murdering of the two harmless and law-abiding citizens. He pictured Contractor McFadden's drive on the fatal morning, and the providential fact that heavy roads made him five minutes late in reaching the scene of the tragedy. Thus was saved the life of the man with large heart and abundant means, who could put upon the track of the murders, the Pinkerton men, whose insignia is "the eye that never sleeps." Through the providence of God, these men had brought the principal in the murder to justice, and the others would soon follow. It was well for the State that this was so. The men in the jury box are Pennsylvanians, and are proud of it, but if these infamous murderers had been left to stalk through the land unpunished, we might well blush for our country. The speaker described Mike as the arch conspirator, the man of courage, who, knowing that he was suspected, sent his confederates out of the country, with the money, thinking to follow and share with them the bloodstained plunder. It is for this terrible crime that we ask you to convict the self-confessed murderer, Michael Rezzolo, the prisoner at the bar, of the highest crime under the law. His murdered victims demands such a conviction at your hands and the law demands it.

CHAPTER XII.

JUDGE RICE CHARGES THE JURY.

Immediately following Captain Darte's telling appeal Judge Rice began his charge to the jury by reminding them that the matter upon which they were to pass was a solemn one, involving a human life. The life of the accused was at stake. He drew attention to the care that had been shown at every stage to see that the defendant as well as the Commonwealth had exact justice. The Court paid a high compliment to the defendant's attorneys, who, without hope of recompense, had devoted their energies in behalf of the prisoner. He then defined the different degrees of murder, and touched upon the amount of weight which should be given to the prisoner's evidence. He read to the jury a part of Mike's confession, and also the corresponding portion of his testimony on the stand. The Court pointed out a number of important circumstances that were proven beyond a matter of doubt. He also charged them that whoever killed Bernard McClure was guilty of murder in the first degree. If they found that Mike did it then such must be their verdict. The subject of principals in the first and second degrees was dwelt upon. If Mike was present at the killing, intentionally, not having fired any of the fatal shots, he was a principal to the murder. The plea that Mike was a participant through fear was touched upon. No threat of bodily harm from Bevevino could justify him in killing an innocent man.

The fact that Chivincci was an accessory after the fact was alleged, and he is now under indictment. His testimony is weakened by this fact, if it tends to screen himself. Mike's confession to Captain Linden was dwelt upon to considerable length. The testimony showed that the promises held out by Thayer were such that any confession made on the strength of such promises was not admissible. Captain Linden testified that after these promises were made, and before Mike's confession was taken down, he had warned Mike that whatever he said would be used against him. If Capt. Linden's words removed the impression made by Thayer's promises,

then the jury should give the written confession due consideration, but not otherwise. The Court drew attention to the fact that Mike's fear of Bevevino rested merely upon Bevevino's unsupported statement to Mike that he had friends in a secret society who would punish any treachery.

The jury, in conclusion, were cautioned not to be influenced by any clamor of public opinion, or by the opinion of any one else. Each man must form his own opinion. It was perfectly right and proper, however, that when they retired to the jury room, they should consult and confer together. The law permitted and expected this. After so doing, they must render their verdict. At 12:20 the jury retired, and the Judge left the bench for a short time, without adjourning Court. Many of the audience, after waiting half an hour, became weary and left. A goodly number remained. Once there was considerable stir, when the Judge entered the room and had the jury called in that he might correct one point in his charge. They then again returned. The jury acted deliberately, electing a foreman, talking over the events of the morning, then came the moment for a decision. One ballot was taken. One ballot was enough.

The jury announced that they had arrived at a verdict. The Judge took the bench, the jury returned to the jury-box, and silence like that of the grave reigned in the court room. The Clerk addressed the jury: "Gentlemen of the jury, have you agreed upon a verdict?"

"We have," replied the foreman.

"What say you? Do you find the prisoner guilty or not guilty?"

The foreman handed to the crier a slip of paper. It was passed to the Judge, who read it deliberately, then handed it to the clerk, with the instruction: Poll the jury.

"Joseph Hart?"

"Here."

"Do you find the prisoner at the bar guilty or not guilty?"

"Guilty!"

"Guilty of what?"

"Guilty of murder in the first degree."

During these proceedings the prisoner had sat in the corner, leaning far down in his

chair, his face flushed and his black eyes glowing like coals. As he heard the awful words he shrank still lower, and for a time seemed crushed by their weight, and his breath came hard. As one a'ter another of the jurymen answered the same interrogatories in similar words, his color left him, and he became pale as the dead.

The jury being all polled, the court thanked them for their work, and they were dismissed. The prisoner was hurried from the court room to be met by a jeering crowd of people who yelled and hooted at Mike as the officers pushed their prisoner through the crowd to the prison van a few feet from the door. A big sigh of relief escaped Mike's lips as the door of the van was safely closed, and he exclaimed, as the van began to move, ''I suppose the people are satisfied now.''

CHAPTER XIII.

MIKE IN JAIL.

Mike's bravado deserted him as soon as he found himself safely locked within his narrow prison cell. The utter hopelessness of his position seemed to dawn upon him as the click of the heavy iron bolts in the wing corridor doors, and the retreating footsteps of the wardens, warned him that his only companions were his fellow prisoners whom, he is aware, have as little sympathy for him as the howling mob outside, who would gladly grace the nearest lamp-post with his wretched body. As the sense of forlorn loneliness breaks upon his obtuse mind the culprit sinks down upon his knees, and in supplicating tones, born of hysterical agony, breaks forth in long and burning appeals to the saints of his native Italy, calling upon them in his mother tongue to appeal to his offended Creator for that mercy that he knows he cannot hope for at the hands of his fellowmen, whose laws of life and property he has so deeply sinned against. Hour after hour he prays and appeals until at last tired nature asserts her domain and the weary head sinks upon the prison cot in pitiful and uneasy slumber.

What visions break in upon his slumbering senses that sway his body to and fro, as though already suspended from the fatal gallows? Does he feel the hangman's rope about his neck, and the fatal trap springing beneath his feet? Is it the belief that already the fatal noose is strangling him, that calls

forth the unearthly yell that resounds down the prison corridors and startles his fellow prisoners from their slumbers and brings the drowsy wardens to their feet with a start? Or was it a vision of young Barney McClure as he looked up from his glassy eyes on the fatal morning when Bevevino placed the rifle near his face and fired a final shot into that kindly brain? Who can tell? Mike could, but will not. He is too deeply immersed in the contemplation of the awful scene to think of explaining to others, as with a groan as of a lost spirit he sinks again into fitful slumber to go through the same blood curdling scenes, that no eyes but his own can see.

"The Mills of the gods grind slowly,

But they grind exceeding fine."

The few miserable days of life that are left to Michael Rezzolo must needs be spent in prayer if he would hope for forgiveness in the life to come, for the law's firm grip is already on his life and the shadow of the gallows is pointing to a new-made grave, that the law's delay may leave unfitted for a few days, but that stern justice will watch over with sleepless eye until all that is mortal of the brutal Italian is safely covered within its gaping depths; and the lives of J. B. McClure and Hugh Flannighan are thus in some small degree, atoned for by the blood of one of the murderous gang who sent them unprepared before the judgment seat of their Creator. Red-nosed Mike must hang.

AGENTS WANTED

TO SELL THIS BOOK.

LIBERAL COMMISSION.

ADDRESS ALL COMMUNICATIONS TO

PUBLISHERS AND *COPYRIGHTERS*

HART & CO.

82 PUBLIC SQ. - WILKES-BARRE, PA.

DO NOT DESTROY THIS CIRCULAR.

Our Agent will call for it.

RED NOSED MIKE,

—— OR ——

THE MOUNTAIN MURDER.

A History of the Crime, Capture, Confession and Trial of the Chief of the Gang who murdered Paymaster McClure and his Body Guard Hugh Flannaghan on the Wilkes-Barre Mountain, on October 19, 1888.

$12.000 in Cash secured by the Italian Railroad Navies employed by Contractor Charles McFadden.

GRAPHICALLY ILLUSTRATED

WITH SCORES OF ENGRAVINGS.

THE story of the Murder and Robbery of Paymaster J. Barney McClure and Hugh Flannaghan on October 19th, last, and the subsequent Capture, Confession and Trial of Red Nosed Mike, in which Pinkerton's men displayed marvelous skill and energy, makes one of the most thrilling stories ever presented to the reading public. We have spared no expense or trouble to fully illustrate and truthfully portray the striking scenes and events of the great Crime and the Trial of the only member of the Banditti now in this country, his companions in Crime having escaped to Italy. The book contains over thirty illustrations, is printed on fine paper, and is of absorbing interest from the begin- . to the end.

PRICE   -   -   25 CENTS.

AGENTS : WANTED.

For Terms, Address

HART & CO.

PUBLISHERS AND COPYRIGHTERS.

(All rights reserved)

82 Public Square, Wilkes-Barre, Pa.